Chapter 2

A Christmas Box That Didn't Match

The young man, still insisting that the freight was not his, followed the agent reluctantly over to the station, accompanied by several of his companions, who had nothing better to do than to see the joke out.

There it was, a box, a bundle, and a packing-case, all labelled plainly and most mysteriously, "Christie W. Bailey, Pine Ridge, Fla."

The man who owned the name could scarcely believe his eyes. He knew of no one who would send him anything. An old neighbor had forwarded the few things he had saved from the sale of the old farm after his father and mother died, and the neighbor had since died himself; so this could not be something forgotten.

He felt annoyed at the arrival of the mystery, and did not know what to do with the things, but at last brought over the wagon and reluctant pony, and with the help of the other men got them loaded on, the pony meanwhile eying his load with dislike and meditating how slow he could make his gait on account of his burden.

Christie Bailey did not wait at the store that night as long as he usually did. He had intended going home by moonlight, but decided to try to make it before the sun went down. He wanted to understand about that freight at once. He found when he went back to the post-office that he could not sit with the same pleasure on a nail-keg and talk as usual. His mind was on the wagon-load. He bought a few things, and started home.

The sun had brought the short winter day suddenly to a close, as it has a habit of doing in Florida, by dropping out of sight and leaving utter darkness with no twilight.

21

Christie lighted an old lantern, and got the things into the cabin at once. Then he took his hatchet and screw-driver, and set to work.

First the packing-case, for he instinctively felt that herein lay the heart of the matter. But not until he had taken the entire front off the case and taken out the handsome organ did he fully realize what had come to him.

More puzzled than ever, he stood back with his arms folded, and whistled. He saw the key attached to a card, and, unlocking the organ, touched gently one of the ivory keys with his rough finger, as one might touch a being from another world.

Then he glanced about to see where he should put it; and suddenly, even in the dull, smoky lamplight, the utter gloom and neglect of the place burst upon him. Without more ado he selected the freest side of the room, and shoved everything out of the way.

Then he brought a broom and swept it clean. After that he set the organ against the wall, and stood back to survey the effect. The disorderly table and the rusty stove were behind him, and the organ gave the spot a strange, cleared-up appearance.

He did not feel at home. He turned to the confusion behind him. Something must be done before he opened anything more. He felt somehow as if the organ was a visitor, and must not see his poor housekeeping.

He seized the frying-pan, scraped the contents into the yard, and called the dog. The dishes he put into a wooden tub outside the door, and pumped water over them. Then the mass of papers and boxes on table and chairs he piled into the darkest corner on the floor, straightened the row of boots and shoes, and, having done all that he could, he came back to the roll and box still unopened.

The roll came first. He undid the strings with awkward fingers, and stood back in admiration once more when he brought to light a thick, bright rug and a Japanese screen.

He spread the rug down, and puzzled some time over the screen, as to its use, but finally stood it up in front of the worst end of the room and began on his box.

There, at last, on the top was a letter in a fine, unknown hand. He opened it slowly, the blood mounting into his face, he knew not why, and read:

"DEAR CHRISTIE:—You see I am so sure you are a girl of my own age that I have concluded to begin my letter informally, and wish you a very merry Christmas and a glad, bright New Year. Of course you may be an old lady or a nice, comfortable, middle-aged one; and then perhaps you will think we are very silly; but we hope and believe you are a girl like ourselves, and so our hearts have opened to you, and we are sending you some things for Christmas."

There followed an account of the afternoon at the freight-station, written in Hazel's most winning way, in which the words and ways and almost the voices and faces of Victoria Landis and Ruth and Esther and Marion and all the rest were shadowed forth.

The color on the young man's face deepened as he read, and he glanced up uneasily at his few poor chairs and miserable couch; then before he read further he went and pulled the screen along to hide more of the confusion.

He read the letter through, his heart waking up to the world and to longings he had never known he possessed before,—to the world in which Christmas has a place and in which young, bright life gives forth glad impulses; read to the end even, where Hazel inscribed her bit of a sermon full of good wishes and a little tender prayer that the spirit of Christmas might reign in that home and that the organ might be a help and a blessing to all around.

There was a pitiful look of almost helpless misery on the young man's face when he had finished. The good old times when God had been a reality were suddenly brought into his reckless, isolated life, and he knew that God was God, even though he had neglected Him so long, and that to-morrow was Christmas Day.

As a refuge from his own thoughts he turned back to the brimming box.

The first article he took out was a pair of dainty knit lavender bedroom slippers with black and white ermine edges and delicate satin bows. Emily Whitten's aunt had knit them for her to take to college with her; and, Emily's feet being many sizes smaller than her aunt supposed, she had never worn them, and had tucked them in at the last minute to make a safe resting-place for a delicate glass vase, which she said would be lovely to hold flowers, on the organ, Sundays.

They had written their nonsense thoughts on bits of labels all over the things, these gay young girls; and the young man read and smiled, and finally laughed aloud. He felt like a little boy just opening his first Christmas stocking.

He unpinned the paper on the couch-cover, and read in Victoria's large, stylish, angular hand full directions for putting it on the couch. He glanced with a twinge of shame at the old lounge, and realized that these gay girls had seen all his shabby belongings and pitied him, and he half-resented the whole thing, until the delight of being pitied and cared for overcame his bitterness, and he laughed again.

Green, soft and restful, had been chosen for the couch-cover; and it could not have fitted better if Victoria Landis had secretly had a tape-measure in her pocket and measured the couch, which perhaps she did on her second trip to the freight-house.

Ruth Summers had made the pillows—there were two of them, and they were large and comfortable and sensible, of harmonizing greens and browns and a gleam of gold here and there.

With careful attention to the directions, the new owner arrayed his old lounge, and placed the pillows as directed, "with a throw and a pat, not *laid* stiffly," from a postscript in Ruth's clear feminine hand. Then he stood back in awe that a thing so familiar and so ugly could suddenly assume such an air of ease and elegance. Would he ever be able to bring the rest of the room up to the same standard?

But the box invited further investigation. There was a bureau set of dainty blue and white, a cover for the top and a pincushion to match. There were also a few yards of the material and a rough sketch with directions for a possible dressing-table, to be made of a wooden box in case Christie had no bureau.

It was from Emily Whitten, and she said she could not remember seeing a bureau among the things, but she was sure any girl would know how to fix one up, and perhaps be glad of some new fixings for it.

At these things the young man looked helplessly, and finally went out into the moonlight, and hunted up an old box which he brushed off with the broom and brought inside, where he clumsily spread out the blue and white frills over its splintery top, and then solemnly tried to stick a pin into the cushion, fumbling in the lapel of his coat for one.

He was growing more and more bewildered with his new possessions, and as each came to light he began to wonder how he was going to be able to entertain and keep up to such a lot of fineries.

Mother Winship had put in a gay knit afghan which looked well over the couch, and next came a layer of Sunday-school singing-books, a Bible, and some lesson leaves. A card said that Esther Wakefield had sent these and she hoped they would be a help in the new Sunday school.

There followed a roll of blackboard cloth, a large cloth map of Palestine, and a box of chalk; and the young man grew more and more helpless. This was worse than the bureau set and the slippers. What was he to do with them all? *He* start a Sunday school! He would be much more likely to start children in the opposite way from heaven if he went on as he had been going the last two years.

His face hardened, and he was almost ready to sweep the whole lot back into the box, nail them up, and send them back where they came from. What did he want of a lot of trash with a set of such burdensome obligations attached?

But curiosity made him go back to see what there was left in the box, and a glance around his room made him unwilling to give up all this luxury.

He looked curiously at the box of fluffy lace things with Marion Halstead's card lying atop. He could only guess that they were some girl's fixings, and he wondered vaguely what he should do with them. Then he unwrapped a photograph of the six girls which had been hurriedly taken and was inscribed, "Guess which is which," with a list of their names written on a circle of paper like spokes to a wheel.

He studied each face with interest, and somehow it was for the writer of the letter that he sought, Hazel Winship. And he thought he should know her at once.

This was going to be very interesting. It would while away some of the long hours when there was nothing worth while to do, and keep him from thinking how long it took orange groves to pay, and what hard luck he had always had.

He decided at first glance that the one in the centre with the clear eyes and firm, sweet mouth was the instigator of all this bounty; and, as his eyes travelled from one face to another and came back to hers each time, he felt more sure of it. There was something frank and pleasant in her gaze. Somehow it would not do to send that girl back her things and tell her he was in no need of her charity. He liked to think she had thought of him, even though she did think of him as a poor discouraged girl or an old mammy.

He stood the picture up against the lace of the pincushion, and forever gave up the idea of trying to send those things back.

There seemed to be one thing more in the bottom of the box, and it was fastened inside another protecting board. He took it at last from its wrappings—a large picture, Hofmann's head of Christ, framed in broad dark Flemish oak to match the tint of the etching.

Dimly he understood who was the subject of the picture, although he had never seen it before. Silently he found a nail and drove it deep into the log of the wall. Just over the organ he hung it, without the slightest hesitation. He had recognized at once where this picture belonged, and knew that it, and not the bright rug, nor the restful couch, nor the gilded screen, nor even the organ itself, was to set the standard henceforth for his home and his life.

He knew this all in an undertone, without its quite coming to the surface of his consciousness. He was weary by this time, with the unusual excitement of the occasion, and much bewildered. He felt like a person suddenly lifted up a little way from the earth and obliged against his will to walk along unsupported in the air.

His mind was in a perfect whirl. He looked from one new thing to another, wondering more and more what they expected of him. The ribbons and lace of the bureau fixings worried him, and the lace collars and pincushion. What had he to do with such? Those foolish little slippers mocked him with a something that was not in his life, a something for which he was not even trying to fit himself. The organ and the books and, above all, the picture seemed to dominate him and demanded of him things which he could never give. A Sunday school! What an absurdity! He!

And the eyes in the picture seemed to look into his soul, and to say, all quietly enough, that He had come here now to live, to take command of his home and its occupant.

He rebelled against it, and turned away from the picture. He seemed to hate all the things, and yet the comfort of them drew him irresistibly.

In sheer weariness at last he put out his light, and, wrapping his old blankets about him, lay down upon the rug; for he would not disturb the couch lest the morning should dawn and his new dream of comfort look as if it had fled away. Besides, how was he ever to get it together again? And, when the morning broke and Christie awoke to the splendor of his things by daylight, the wonder of it all dawned, too, and he went about his work with the same spell still upon him.

Now and again he would raise his eyes to the pictured Christ and drop them again, reverently. It seemed to him this morning as if that Presence were living and had come to him in spite of all his railings at fate, his bitterness and scoffing, and his feckless life. It seemed to say with that steady gaze: "What will you do with me? I am here, and you cannot get away from my drawing."

It was not as if his life had been filled formerly with tradition and teaching; for his mother had died when he was a little fellow, and the thin-lipped, hard-working maiden aunt who had cared for him in her place, whatever religion she might have had in her heart, never thought it necessary to speak it out beyond requiring a certain amount of decorum on Sunday and regular attendance at Sunday school.

In Sunday school it had been his lot to be under a good elder who read the questions from a lesson leaf and looked helplessly at the boys who were employing their time in more pleasurable things the while. The very small amount of holy things he had absorbed from his days at Sunday schools had failed to leave him with a strong idea of the love of God or any adequate knowledge of the way to be saved.

In later years, of course, he had listened listlessly to preaching; and, when he went to college—a small, insignificant one,—he had come in contact with religious people; but here, too, he had heard as one hears a thing in which one has not the slightest interest.

He had gathered and held this much, that the God in whom the Christian world believed was holy and powerful, and the most of the world were culprits. Heretofore God's love had passed him by unaware.

Now the pictured eyes of the Son of God seemed to breathe out tenderness and yearning. For the first time in his life a thought of the possibility of love between his soul and God came to him.

His work that morning was much more complicated than usual. He wasted little time in getting breakfast. He had to clean house. He could not bear the idea that the old régime and the new should touch shoulders as they did behind that screen. So with broom and scrubbing-brush he went to work.

He had things in pretty good shape at last, and was just coming in from giving the horse a belated breakfast when a strange impulse seized him.

At his feet, creeping all over the white sand in delicate tracery, were wild pea blossoms, crimson, white, and pink. He had never noticed them before. What were they but weeds? But with a new insight into possibilities in art, he stooped and gathered a few of them, and, holding them awkwardly, went into the house to put them into his new vase. He felt half-ashamed of them, and held them behind him as he entered; but with the shame there mingled an eagerness to see how they would look in the vase on the "blue bureau thing,"

> " 'Will you walk into my parlor?'
> Said the spider to the fly,
> 'Tis the prettiest little parlor
> That ever you did spy,' "

sang out a rich tenor voice in greeting.

"I say, Chris! What are you setting up for? What does it all mean? Ain't going to get married or nothing, are you, man? because I'll be obliged to go to town and get my best coat out of pawn if you are."

"Aw, now that is gweat!" drawled another voice, English in its accents. "Got anything good to dwink? Twot it out, and we'll be better able to appweciate all this lugshuwy!"

Chapter 3

"And What Are You Going to Say to Her?"

The young man felt a rising tendency to swear. He had forgotten all about the fellows and their agreement to meet and have the day out in jollification. So great had been the spell upon him that he had forgotten to put the little feminine things away from curious eyes.

There he stood foolishly in the middle of his own floor, a bunch of "weeds" in his hand which he had not the sense to drop, while afar the sound of a cracked church bell gave a soft reminder, which the distant popping of firecrackers at a cabin down the road confirmed, that this was Christmas Day. Christmas Day, and the face of the Christ looking down at him tenderly from his own wall.

The oath that was rising to his lips at his foolish plight was stayed. He could not take that name in vain with those eyes upon him. The spell was not broken even yet.

With a sudden quick settling of his lips, he threw back his head, daring in his eyes, and walked over to the glass vase to fill it with water. It was like him to brave it out and tell the whole story now that he was caught.

He was a broad-shouldered young man, firmly knit, with a head well set on his shoulders, and but for a certain careless slouch in his gait might have been fine to look upon. His face was not handsome, but he had good brown eyes with deep hazel lights in them that kindled when he looked at you.

His hair was red, deep and rich, and decidedly curly. His gestures were strong and regular. If there had not been a certain hardness about his face he would have been interesting, but that look made one turn away disappointed.

His companions were both big men like himself. The Englishman—one of that large class of second or third sons with a

31

good education and a poor fortune, and very little practical knowledge how to better it, so many of whom come to Florida to try orange-growing—was loose-jointed and awkward, with pale blue eyes, hay-colored hair, and a large jaw with loose lips. The other was handsome and dark, with a weak mouth and daring black eyes which continually warred with one another.

Both were dressed in rough clothes, trousers tucked into boots with spurs, dark flannel shirts, and soft riding-hats. The Englishman wore gloves and affected a certain loud style in dress. They carried their riding-whips, and walked undismayed upon the bright colors of the rug.

"O, I say now, get off there with those great clods of boots, can't you?" exclaimed Christie, with a sudden descent of housewifely carefulness. "Anybody'd think you'd been brought up in a barn, Armstrong."

Armstrong put on his eye-glasses,—he always wore them as if they were a monocle,—and examined the rug carefully.

"Aw, I beg pawdon! Awfully nice, ain't it? Sorry I didn't bwing my patent leathers along. Wemind me next time, please, Mawtimer."

Christie told the story of his Christmas gifts in as few words as possible. Somehow he did not feel like elaborating it.

The guests seized upon the photograph of the girls, and became hilarious over it.

"Takes you for a girl, does she?" said Mortimer. "That's great! Which one is she? I choose that fine one with snapping black eyes and handsome teeth. She knew her best point, or she wouldn't have laughed when her picture was taken."

Victoria Landis's eyes would have snapped indeed, could she have heard the comments upon herself and the others; but she was safe out of hearing, far up in the North.

The comments went on most freely. Christie found himself disgusted with his friends. Only yesterday he would have laughed at all they said, and now what made the difference? Was it that letter? Would the other fellows feel the same if he should read it to them?

But he never would! The red blood stole up in his face. He could hear their shouts of laughter now over the tender little girlish phrases. It should not be desecrated. He was glad indeed that he had put it in his coat pocket the night before.

There seemed to be a sacredness about the letter and the pictures and all the things, and it went against the grain to hear the coarse laughter of his friends.

At last they began to speak about the girl in the centre of the group, the clear-eyed, firm-mouthed one whom he had selected for Hazel. His blood boiled. He could stand it no longer. With one sweep of his long, strong arm he struck the picture from them with "Aw, shut up! You make me tired!" and, picking it up, put it in his pocket.

Whereat the fun of his companions took a new turn. It suited their fancy to examine the toilet-table decked out in blue and lace. The man named Mortimer knew the lace collars and handkerchiefs for woman's attire, and they turned upon their most unwilling host and decked him in fine array.

He sat helpless and mad, with a large lace collar over his shoulders, and another hanging down in front arranged over the bureau-cover, which was spread across him as a background, while a couple of lace-bordered handkerchiefs adorned his head.

"And what are you going to say to her for all these pretty presents, Christie, my girl?" laughed Mortimer.

"Say to her!" gasped Christie.

It had not occurred to him before that it would be necessary to say anything. A horrible oppression seemed to be settling down upon his chest. He wished that the whole array of things were back in their boxes and on their way to their ridiculous owners. He got up, and kicked at the rug, and tore the lace finery from his neck, stumbling on the lavender bedroom slippers which his tormentors had stuck on the toes of his shoes.

"Why, certainly, man,—I beg your pardon,—*my dear girl*—" went on Mortimer. "You don't intend to be so rude as not to reply, or say, 'I thank you very kindly'!"

Christie's thick auburn brows settled into a scowl, but the attention of the others was drawn to the side of the room where the organ stood.

"That's awfully fine, don't you know?" remarked Armstrong,

levelling his eye-glasses at the picture. "It's by somebody gweat, I dawn just wemembah who."

"Fine frame," said Mortimer tersely as he opened the organ and sat down before it.

And the new owner of the picture felt for the first time in his acquaintance with these two men that they were somehow out of harmony with him.

He glanced up at the picture with the color mounting in his face, half pained for the friendly gaze that had been so lightly treated. He did not in the least understand himself.

But the fingers touching the keys now were not altogether unaccustomed. A soft, sweet strain broke through the room, and swelled louder and fuller until it seemed to fill the little log house and be wafted through the open windows to the world outside.

Christie stopped in his walk across the room, held by the music. It seemed the full expression of all he had thought and felt during the last few hours.

A few chords, and the player abruptly reached out to the pile of singing-books above him, and, dashing the book open at random, began playing, and in a moment in a rich, sweet tenor sang. The others drew near, and each took a book and joined in.

> "He holds the key of all unknown,
>   And I am glad;
> If other hands should hold the key,
> Or if He trusted it to me,
>   I might be sad."

The song was a new creed spoken to Christie's soul by a voice that seemed to fit the eyes in the picture. What was the matter with him? He did not at all know. His whole life seemed suddenly shaken.

It may be that the fact of his long residence alone in that desolate land, with but few acquaintances, had made him more ready to be swayed by this sudden stirring of new thoughts and feelings. Certain it was that Christie Bailey was not acting like himself.

But the others were interested in the singing. It had been long since they had had an instrument to accompany them, and they enjoyed the sound of their own voices. They would have preferred, perhaps, a book of college songs, or, better still, the latest street songs; but, as they were not at hand, and "Gospel Hymns" were, they found pleasure even in these.

On and on they sang, through hymn after hymn, their voices growing stronger as they found pieces which had in them some hint of familiarity.

The music filled the house, and floated out into the bright summer Christmas world outside; and presently Christie felt rather than saw a movement at the window, and, looking up, beheld it dark with little, eager faces of the black children. Their supply of firecrackers having given out, they had sought for further celebration, and had been drawn with delight by the unusual sounds. Christie dropped into a chair and gazed at them in wonder, his eyes growing troubled and the frown deepening. He could not make it out. Here he had been for some time, and these little children had never ventured to his premises. Now here they were in full force, their faces fairly shining with delight, their eyes rolling with wonder and joy over the music.

It seemed a fulfilment of the prophecy of the letter that had come with the organ. He began to tremble at the thought of the possibilities that might be entailed upon him with his newly acquired and unsought-for property. And yet he could not help a feeling of pride that all these things were his and that a girl of such evident refinement and cultivation had taken the trouble to send them. To be sure, she wouldn't have done it at all if she had had any idea who or what he was, but that did not matter. She did not know, and she never would know.

He saw the children's curious eyes wander over the room and rest here and there delighted, and his own eyes followed theirs. How altogether nice it was! What a desolate hole it had been before! How was it he had not noticed?

Amid all these thoughts the concert came suddenly to a close. The organist turned upon his stool, and, addressing the audience in the window, remarked, with a good many flourishes: "That finishes the programme for to-day, dear friends. Allow me to announce that a Sunday school will be held in this place on next Sunday afternoon at half-past two o'clock, at which you are all invited to be present.

Do you understand? Half-past two. And bring your friends. Now will you all come?"

Amid many a giggle and a bobbing of round black heads they answered as one boy and one girl, "Yes, sah!" and went rollicking down the road in haste to spread the news, their bare feet flying through the sand, and vanished as they had come.

Chapter 4

"A Letter That Wrote Itself"

"What did you do that for?" thundered Christie, suddenly realizing what would be the outcome of this performance.

"Don't speak so loud, Christie, dear; it isn't ladylike, you know. I was merely saving you the trouble of announcing the services. You'll have a good attendance, I'm sure, and we'll come and help you out with the music," said Mortimer in a sweetly unconscious tone.

Christie came at him with clenched fist, which he laughingly dodged, and went on bantering. But the two young men soon left, for Christie was angry and was not good company. They tried to coax him off to meet some of their other boon companions, but he answered shortly, "No," and they left him to himself.

Left alone, he was in no happy frame of mind. He had intended to go with them. There would be something good to eat, and of course something to drink, and cards, and a jolly good time all around. He could forget for a little while his hard luck, and the slowness of the oranges, and his own wasted life, and feel some of the joy of living. But he had the temper that went with his hair, and now nothing would induce him to go.

Was it possible there was something else, too, holding him back? A subtle something which he did not understand, somehow connected with the letter and the picture and the organ?

Well, if there was, he did not stop to puzzle it out. Instead, he threw himself down on the newly arrayed couch, and let his head sink on one of those delightfully soft pillows, and tried to think.

He took out the letter, and read it over again.

When he read the sentences about praying for him, there came a choking sensation in his throat such as he had not felt since the time he nearly drowned, and realized that there was no mother any more to go to. This girl wrote as a mother might perhaps talk, if one had a mother.

He folded the letter, and put it back in his pocket; and then, closing and locking the door, he sat down at the organ and tried to play it.

As he knew nothing whatever about music, he did not succeed very well, and he turned from it with a sigh to look up at those pictured eyes once more and find them following his every movement. Some pictures have that power of seeming to follow one around the room.

Christie got up and walked away, still looking at the picture, and turned and came back again.

Still the eyes seemed to remain upon his face with that strong, compelling gaze. He wondered what it meant, and yet he was glad it had come. It seemed like a new friend.

Finally he sat down and faced the question that was troubling him. He must write a letter to that girl—to those girls, and he might as well have done with it at once and get it out of the way. After that he could feel he had paid the required amount, and could enjoy his things. But it simply was not decent not to acknowledge their receipt. But the tug of war was to know how to do it.

Should he confess that he was a young man and not the Christie they had thought, and offer to send back the things for them to confer upon a more worthy subject?

He glanced hastily about on his new belongings with sudden dismay. Could he give up all this? No. He would not.

His eyes caught the pictured eyes once more. He had found a friend and a little comfort. It had come to him unbidden. He would not bid it depart.

Besides, it would only make those kind people most uncomfortable. They would think they had been doing something dreadful to send a young man presents, especially one whom they had never seen. He knew the ways of the world, a little. And that Hazel Winship who had written the letter, she was a charming person. He would not like to spoil her pretty dream of his being a friendless girl. Let her keep her fancies; they could do no harm.

He would write and thank her as if he were the girl they all supposed him. He had always been good at playing a part or imitating any one; he would just write the letter in a girlish hand—it would not be hard to do—and thank them as they expected to be thanked by another girl. That would be the end of it. Then, when his oranges came into bearing,—if they ever did,—he would send them each a box of oranges anonymously, and all would be right.

As for that miserable business Mortimer had got him into, he would fix that up by shutting up the house and riding away early Sunday morning, and the children might come to Sunday school to their hearts' content. He would not be there to be bothered or bantered.

In something like a good humor he settled to his task.

He wrote one or two formal notes, and tore them up. As he looked about on the glories of his room, he began to feel that such thanks were inadequate to express his feelings. Then he settled to work once more, and began to be interested.

"My dear unknown Friend," he wrote, "I scarcely know how to begin to thank you for the kindness you have showered upon me."

He read the sentence over, and decided it sounded very well and not at all as if a man had written it. The spirit of fun took possession of him, and he made up his mind to write those girls a good long letter, and tell them all about his life, only tell it just as if he were a girl. It would while away this long, unoccupied day. He wrote on:

"You wanted to know all about me; so I am going to tell you. I do not, as you suppose, teach school. I had a little money from the sale of father's farm after he died, and I put it into some land down here planted to young orange-trees. I had heard a great deal about how much money was to be made in orange-growing, and thought I would like to try it. I am all alone in the world—not a soul who cares in the least about me, and so there was no one to advise me against it.

"I came down here and boarded at first, but found it would be a good thing for me to live among my trees, so I could look after things better; so I had a little cabin built of logs right in the grove, and sent for all the old furniture that had been saved from the old home, which was not much, as most things had been sold with the house. You saw how few and poor they were.

"It seems so strange to think that you, who evidently have all the good things of the world to make you happy, should have stopped to think and take notice of poor, insignificant me. It is wonderful, more wonderful than anything that ever happened to me in all my life. I look about on my beautified room, and cannot believe it is I.

"I live all alone in my log cabin, surrounded by a lot of young trees which seem to me very slow in doing anything to make me rich. If I had known all I know now, I never would have come here; but one has to learn by experience, and I'll just have to stick now until something comes of it.

"I am not exactly a girl just like yourselves as you say; for I am twenty-eight years old, and, to judge by your pictures, there isn't one of you as old as that. You are none of you over twenty-two, I am sure, if you are that.

"Besides, you are all beautiful girls, while I most certainly am not. To begin with, my hair is red, and I am brown and freckled from the sun and wind and rain; and, in fact, I am what is called homely. So you see it is not as serious a matter for me to live all alone down here in an orange-grove as it would be for one of you. I have a strong little pony who carries me on his back or in my old buckboard, and does the ploughing. What work I cannot do myself about the grove, I hire done, of course. I also have a few chickens and a dog.

"If you could have seen my little house the night your boxes arrived and were unpacked, you would appreciate the difference the things you have sent make in my surroundings. But you can never know what a difference they will make in my life."

Here the rapid pen halted, and the writer wondered whether that might be a prophecy. So far, he reflected, he had written nothing but what was strictly true; and yet he had not made known his identity.

This last sentence seemed to be writing itself, for he really had no idea that the change in his room would make much difference in his life, except to add a little comfort. He raised his eyes; and, as they met those in the picture, it seemed to be forced upon him that there was to be a difference, and somehow he was not sorry. The old life was not attractive, but he wondered what it would be. He felt as if he were standing off watching the developments in his own life as one might watch the life of the hero in a story.

There was one more theme in Hazel Winship's letter which he had not touched upon, he found, after he had gone over each article by name and said nice things about them all and what a lot of comfort he would have from them.

He was especially pleased with his sentence about the bedroom slippers and lace collars. "They are much too fine and pretty to be worn," he had written, "especially by such a large, awkward person as I am; but I like to feel them and see them, and think how pretty they would look on some of the dainty, pretty girls who sent them to me."

But all the time he was reading his letter over he felt that something would have to be said on that other subject. At last he started in again:

"There is a cabin down the road a little way, and this morning a friend of mine came in and played a little while on the organ—I can't play myself, but I am going to learn"—he had not thought about learning before, but now he knew he should—"and we all got to singing out of the books you sent. By and by I looked up, and saw the doorway full of little ragamuffins listening for all they were worth. I presume I shall be able to give them a good deal of pleasure listening to that organ sometimes, though I am afraid I wouldn't be much of a hand at starting a Sunday school"—that sentence sounded rather mannish for a girl of twenty-eight; but he had to let it stand, as he could think of nothing better to say—"as I never knew much about such things. Though I'm much obliged for your praying, I'm sure. It will give me a pleasant feeling at night when I'm all alone to know some one in the world is thinking about me, and I'm sure if prayers can do any good yours ought to.

"But about the Sunday school, I don't want to disappoint you after you've been so kind to send all the papers and books. Maybe I could give the black children some of the papers, and let them study the lessons out for themselves; and I used to be quite a hand at drawing once. I might practise up and draw them some pictures to amuse them sometime when they come around again. I'll do my best.

"I like to think of you all at college having a good time. My school days were the best of my life. I wish I could go over them again. I have a lot of books; but, when I come in tired at night, it seems so lonely here, and I'm so tired I just go to sleep. It doesn't seem to make much difference about my reading any more, anyway. The oranges won't know it. They grow just as soon for me as if I kept up with the procession.

"I appreciate your kindness, though I don't know how to tell you how deeply it has touched me. I have picked out the one in the middle, the girl with the laughing eyes, and a sweet, firm mouth, and the loveliest expression I ever saw on any face, to be Miss Hazel Winship, the one who thought of this whole beautiful plan. Am I right? I'll study the others up later.

"Yours very truly—" here he paused, and, carefully erasing the last word, wrote "lovingly,"

"CHRISTIE W. BAILEY."

He sat back, and covered his face with his hands. A queer, glad feeling had come over him while he was writing those things about Hazel Winship. He wondered what it was. He actually enjoyed saying those things to her and knowing she would be pleased to read them, and not think him impertinent.

And he had written a good many promises, after all. What led him on to that? Did he mean to keep them? Yes, he believed he did; only those fellows, Armstrong and Mortimer, should not know anything about it. He would carry out his plan of going away Sundays until those ridiculous fellows forgot their nonsense. And, so thinking, he folded and addressed his letter.

A little more than a week later six girls gathered in a cosey college room—Hazel's—to hear the letter read.

"You see," said Hazel, with triumphant light in her eyes, "I was right; she is a girl like us. It doesn't matter in the least little bit that she is twenty-eight. That isn't old. And for once I am glad you see that my impulses are not always crazy. I am going to send this letter home at once to father and mother. They were really quite troublesome about this. They thought it was the wildest thing I ever did, and I've been hearing from it all vacation. Now listen!"

And Hazel read the letter amid many interruptions.

"I'll tell you what it is, girls," she said, as she finished the letter;

"we must keep track of her now we've found her. I'm so glad we did it. She isn't a Christian, that's evident; and we must try to make her into one, and work through her a Sunday school. That would be a work worth while. Then maybe sometime we can have her up here for a winter, and give her a change. Wouldn't she enjoy it? It can't be this winter, because we'll have to work so hard here in college we'd have no time for anything else; but after we have all graduated wouldn't it be nice? I'll tell you what I'd like to do; I'd like the pleasure of taking Christie Bailey to Europe. I know she would enjoy it. Just think what fun it would be to watch her eyes shine over new things. I don't mind her red hair one bit. Red-haired people are lovely if they know how to dress to harmonize with their complexions."

"How fortunate we used green for that couch-cover! Christie's hair will be lovely against it," murmured Victoria, in a serio-comic tone, while all the girls set up a shout at Hazel's wild flights of fancy.

"Take Christie Bailey to Europe! O, Hazel! I'm afraid you will be simply dreadful, now you have succeeded in one wild scheme. You will make us do all sorts of things, and never stop at reason."

Hazel's cheeks flushed. It always hurt her a little that these girls did not go quite as far in her philanthropic ideas as she did herself. She had quite taken this Christie girl into her heart, and she wanted them all to do the same.

"Well, girls, you must all write to her, anyway, and encourage her. Think what it would be to be down there, a girl, all alone, and raising oranges. I think she is a hero!"

"O, we'll all write, of course," said Victoria, with mischief in her eye; "but call her a heroine, do, Hazel."

And they all did write, letters full of bright nonsense, and sweet, tender, chatty letters, and letters full of girlish pity, attempts to make life more bearable to the poor girl all alone down in Florida. But a girl who confesses to being homely and red-haired and twenty-eight cannot long hold a prominent place in the life of any but an enthusiast such as Hazel was, and very soon the other five letters dropped off, and Christie Bailey was favored with but one correspondent from that Northern college.

* * *

But to return to Florida. That first Sunday morning after Christmas, everything did not go just as was planned by Christie.

In the first place, he overslept. He had discovered some miserable scales on some of his most cherished trees, and he had had to trudge to town Saturday morning,—the man was using the pony ploughing,—and get some whale-oil soap, and then spend the rest of the day until dark spraying his trees. It was no wonder that he was too tired to wake early the next day.

Then, when he finally went out to the pony, he discovered that he was suffering from a badly cut foot, probably the result of the careless hired man and a barbed-wire fence. The swollen foot needed attention.

The pony made comfortable, he reflected on what he would do next. To ride on that pony away anywhere was impossible. To walk he was not inclined. The sun was warm for that time of year, and he still felt stiff from his exertions of the day before. He concluded he would shut up the house, and lie down, and keep still when any one came to call, and they would think him away.

With this purpose in view he gave the pony and the chickens a liberal supply of food, that he need not come out again till evening, and went into the house; but he had no more than reached there when he heard a loud knocking at the front door, evidently with the butt end of a whip; and before he could decide what to do it was thrown open, and Mortimer and Armstrong entered, another young Englishman following close behind. Armstrong wore shiny patent-leather shoes, and seemed anxious to make them apparent.

"Good mawning, Miss Bailey," he said, affably. "Glad to see you looking so fresh and sweet. We just called round to help you pwepare for your little Sunday school."

Chapter 5

A Sunday School in Spite of Itself

Christie was angry. He stood still, looking from one to another of his three guests like a wild animal at bay. They knew he was angry, and that fact contributed not a little to their enjoyment. They meant to carry out the joke to the end.

The third man, Rushforth by name, stood grinning in the rear of the other two. The joke had been so thoroughly explained to him that he could fully appreciate it. He was not noted for being quick at a joke. Armstrong, however, seemed to have a full sense of the ridiculous.

Firmly and cheerfully they took their way with Christie; and he, knowing that resistance was futile, sat down upon his couch in glum silence, and let them work their will.

"I stopped on the way over, and reminded our friends in the cabin below that the hour was two-thirty," remarked Mortimer, as he took a large dinner-bell from his side pocket and rang a note or two. "That's to let them know the time when we are ready to 'take up.'"

Christie scowled, and the others laughted uproariously.

"Now, Armstrong, you and I will go out and reconnoitre for seats, while Rushforth stays here and helps this dear girl dust her parlor ornaments and brickbats. We'll need plenty of seats, for we'll have quite a congregation if all I've asked turn out."

They came back in a few minutes laden with boxes and boards which they ranged in three rows across the end of the cabin facing the organ.

Christie sat and glared at them.

He was very angry, and was trying to think whether to bear it out and see what they would do next, or run away to the woods. He had little doubt that if he should attempt the latter they would all three follow him, and perhaps bind him to a seat to witness the performances they had planned; for they were evidently "taking it out of him" for having all this luxury and not taking them into the innermost confidences of his heart about it.

He shut his teeth and wondered what Hazel would say if she knew how outrageously her idea of a Sunday school was going to be burlesqued.

Armstrong tacked up the blackboard, and got out the chalk. Then, discovering the folded cloth map of the Holy Land, he tacked that up at the end wall where all could see it. Mortimer mapped out the programme.

"Now, Rushforth, you pass the books and the lesson leaves, and I'll stay at the organ and preside. Miss Christie's a little shy about speaking out to-day, you see, and we'll have to help her along before we put her in the superintendent's place. Christie, you can make some pictures on the blackboard. Anything'll do. This is near Christmas—you can make Santa Claus coming down the chimney if you like. I'll run the music, and we'll have quite a time of it. We'll be able to tell the fellows all about it down at the lake next week, and I shouldn't wonder if we'd have a delegation over from Mulberry Creek next Sunday to hear Elder Bailey speak—I beg pardon; I mean Miss Bailey. You must excuse me, dear; on account of your freckles I sometimes take you for a man."

Mortimer spread open a Bible that had come with the singing-books, and actually found the place in the lesson leaf, and made them listen while he read, and declared that Christie ought to give a talk on the lesson. And thus they carried on their banter the whole morning long.

Christie sat glowering in the corner.

He could not make up his mind what to do. For some strange reason he did not want a Sunday school caricatured in his house and with that picture looking down upon it all, and yet he did not know why he didn't want it. He had never been squeamish before about such things. The fellows would not understand it, and he did not understand it himself. But it went against the grain.

Now as it came on about dinner-time he thought they would perhaps go if he offered no refreshments; but no; they seemed to have no such idea. Instead, they sent Armstrong outside to their light wagon they had tied at the tree by the roadside, and he came back laden with a large basket which they proceeded to unpack.

There were canned meats and jellies and pickles and baked beans and all sorts of canned goods that have to be substituted for the genuine article in Florida, where fresh meat and vegetables are not always to be had.

Armstrong went out again, and this time came back with a large case of bottles.

He set it down with a thump on the floor just opposite the picture, while he shut the door. The clink of the bottles bespoke a hilarious hour, and carried memories of many a time of feasting in which Christie had participated before.

His face crimsoned as if some honored friend had suddenly been brought to look upon the worst of his hard, careless life, and he suddenly rose with determination. Here was something which he could not stand.

He drank sometimes, it is true. The fellows all knew it. But both he and they knew that the worst things they had ever done in their lives had been done and said under the influence of liquor. They all had memories of wild debauches of several days' duration, when they had been off together and had not restrained themselves. Each one knew his own heart's shame after such a spree as this. Each knew the other's shame. They never spoke about it, but it was one of the bonds that bound them together, these drunken riots of theirs, when they put their senses at the service of cards and wine, and never stopped until the liquor had given out. At such times each knew that he would have sold his soul for one more penny to stake at the game, or one more drink, had the devil been about in human form to bid for it.

They were none of them drunkards, few of them even constant drinkers, partly because they had little money to spend in such a habit. They all had strong bodies able to endure much, and their life out-of-doors did not tend to create unnatural cravings of appetite. Rather had they forced themselves into these revelries as a means of amusing themselves in a land where there was little but work to fill up the long months and years of waiting.

This case of liquor was not the first that had been in Christie's cabin. He had never felt before that it was out of place in entering there; but now the picture hung there, and the case of liquor, representing the denial of God, seemed to Christie a direct insult to the One whose presence had in a mysterious way crept into the cabin with the picture.

Also he saw at a flash what the fellows were planning to do. They knew his weakness. They remembered how skilled his tongue was in turning phrases when loosened by intoxicants. They were planning to get him drunk—perhaps had even drugged some of the bottles slightly—and then to make him talk, and even pray, it might be!

At another time this might have seemed funny to him. He had not realized before how far he had been going in the way from truth and righteousness. But now his whole soul rose up in loathing of himself, his ways, and his companions.

A sentence of his mother's prayer for him when he was but a little child that had not been in his mind for years now came as clear as if a voice had spoken it in his ear, "God make my little Chris a good man!"

And this was how it had been answered. Poor mother!

What Hazel Winship would think of the scene also flashed into his mind. He strode across that room in his angry strength before his astonished companions could stop him; and, taking that case of liquor in his muscular arms, he dashed it far out the open door across the road and into the woods. Then he turned back to the three amazed men.

"You won't have any of that stuff in here!" he said firmly. "If you're bound to have a Sunday school, a Sunday school we'll have; but we won't have any drunken men at it. Perhaps you enjoy mixing things up that way, but I'm not quite a devil yet."

They had not known there was such strength in him. He looked fairly splendid as he stood there in the might of right, his deep eyes glowing darker brown and every mahogany curl a-tremble with determination.

"Aw! Certainly! Beg pawdon!" said Armstrong, settling his eyeglasses that he might observe his former friend more closely. "I meant no hawm, I'm suah." Armstrong was always polite. If an earthquake had thrown him to the ground, he would have arisen and said, "Aw! I beg pawdon!"

But Christie was master in his own house. The others exclaimed a little, and tried to joke him upon his newly acquired temperance principles; but he would not open his lips further on the subject, and they ate their canned meats and jellies and bread moistened only by water from Christie's pump in the yard.

They had scarcely finished when the first instalment of the Sunday school arrived in faded but freshly starched calicoes laundered especially for the occasion. They pattered to the door barefooted, clean, and shining, followed by some of their elders, who lingered smiling and shy at the gateway, uncertain whether to credit the invitation to "Mr. Christie's" cabin. Mr. Christie had never been so hospitable before. But the children, spying the rudely improvised benches, crept in, and the others followed.

Christie stood scowling in the back end of the cabin. Sunday school was on his hands. He could not help it any more than he could help the coming of the organ and the picture. It was a part of his new possessions.

He felt determined that it should not be a farce. How he was going to prevent it he did not know, but he meant to do it.

He looked up at the picture again. It seemed to give him strength. Of course it was but fancy that it had seemed to smile approval after he had flung that liquor out the door; but in spite of his own reason he could not but feel that the Man of the picture was enduring insult here in his house, and that he must fight for His sake.

Added to that was Hazel Winship's faith in him and her desire for a Sunday school. His honor was at stake. He would never have gone out and gathered up a Sunday school to nurse into life, even for Hazel Winship. Neither would he have consented to help in one if his permission had been asked; but now, when it was, as it were, thrust upon him, like a little foundling child all smiling and innocent of possible danger to it, what could he do but help it out?

They were all seated now, and a hush of expectancy pervaded the room.

The three conspirators over by the organ were consulting and laughing in low tones.

Christie knew that the time had come for action. He raised his eyes to the picture once more. To his fancy the eyes seemed to smile assurance to him as he went forward to the organ.

Christie quietly took up a singing-book, and, opening at random, said, "Let us sing number one hundred and thirty-four." He was surprised when they began to sing to find it was the same song that Mortimer had sung first on Christmas morning.

His three friends turned in astonishment toward him. They began to think he was entering into the joke like his own old self, but instead there was a grave, earnest look on his face they had never seen there before.

Mortimer put his fingers on the keys, and began at once. Christie seemed to have taken the play out of their hands and turned the tables upon them. They began to wonder what he would do next. This was fine acting on his part, they felt, for him to take the predicament in which they had placed him and work it out in earnest.

The song was almost finished, and still Christie did not know what to do next.

He announced another hymn at random, and watched old Aunt Tildy settle her steel-bowed spectacles over her nose and fumble among the numbers. The Sunday school was entering into the music with zest. The male trio who led were singing with might and main, but with an amused smile on their faces as if they expected developments soon.

Just then an aged black man came hobbling in. His hair and whiskers were white, and his worn Prince Albert coat ill fitted his bent figure; but there was a clerical manner which clung to the old coat and gave Christie hope. When the song was finished, he raised his eyes without any hesitation and spoke clearly.

"Uncle Moses," he said, "we want to begin right, and you know all about Sunday schools; can't you give us a start?"

Uncle Moses slowly took off his spectacles, and put them carefully away in his pocket while he cleared his throat.

"I ain't much on speechifyin', Mistah Bailey," said he; "but I kin pray. 'Kase you see when I's talkin' to God den I ain't thinkin' of my own sinful, stumblin' speech."

The choir did not attempt to restrain their risibles, but Christie was all gravity.

"That's it, Uncle. That's what we need. You pray." It came to him to wonder for an instant whether Hazel Winship was praying for her Sunday school then, too.

All during the prayer Christie wondered at himself. He conduct-
ing a religious service in his own house and asking somebody to
pray! And yet, as the trembling, pathetic sentences rolled out, he felt
glad that homage was being rendered to the Presence that seemed to
have been in the room ever since the picture came.

"O our Father in heaven, we is all poh sinnahs!" said Uncle
Moses, earnestly, and Christie felt it was true, himself among the
number. It was the first prayer that the young man ever remembered to have felt all the way through. "We is all sick and miserable
with the disease of sin. We's got it *bad,* Lord"—here Christie felt the
seat behind him shake. Mortimer was behaving very badly. "But,
Lord," went on the quavering old voice, "we know dere's a remedy.
Away down in Palestine, in de Holy Land, in an Irish shanty, was
where de fust medicine-shop of de world was set up, an' we been
gettin' de good ob it eber sence. O Lord, we praise thee to-day for de
little chile dat lay in dat manger a long time ago, dat brung de fust
chance of healing to us poh sinners—"

Mortimer could scarcely contain himself, and the two
Englishmen were laughing on general principles. Christie raised his
bowed head, and gave Mortimer a warning shove, and they sub-
sided somewhat; but the remarkable prayer went on to its close, and
to Christie it seemed to speak a new gospel, familiar, and yet never
comprehended before. Could it be that these poor, ignorant people
were to teach him a new way?

By the time the prayer was over, he had lost his trepidation. The
spirit of it had put a determination into him to make this gathering
a success, not merely for the sake of foiling his tormentors, but for
the sake of the trusting, childlike children who had come there in
good faith.

He felt a little exultant thrill as he thought of Hazel Winship and
her commission. He would try to do his best for her sake to-day at
least, whatever came of it in future. Neither should those idiots behind him have a grand tale of his breaking down in embarrassment
to take away to the fellows over at the lake.

Summoning all his daring, he gave out another hymn, which
happened fortunately to be familiar to the audience, and to have
many verses; and he reached for a lesson leaf.

O, if his curiosity had but led him to examine the lesson for to-day, or any lesson, in fact! He must say something to carry things off, and he must have a moment to consider. The words swam before his eyes. He could make nothing out of it all.

Dared he ask one of the fellows to read the Scripture lesson while he prepared his next line of action?

He looked at them. They were an uncertain quantity, but he must have time to think a minute. Armstrong was the safest. His politeness would hold him within bounds.

When the song finished, he handed the leaflet to Armstrong, saying, briefly, "You read the verses, Armstrong."

Armstrong in surprise answered, "Aw, certainly," and adjusting his eye-glasses, began, "Now when Jesus was bawn in Bethlehem—"

"Hallelujah!" interjected Uncle Moses, with his head thrown back and his eyes closed. He was so happy to be in a meeting once more.

"Aw! I beg pahdon, suh! What did you say?" said Armstrong, looking up innocently.

This came near to breaking up the meeting, at least, the white portion of it; but Christie, a gleam of determination in his eye because he had caught a little thread of a thought, said gruffly: "Go on, Armstrong. Don't mind Uncle Moses."

When the reading was over, Christie, annoyed by the actions of his supposed helpers, seized a riding-whip from the corner of the room and came forward to where the map of Palestine hung. As he passed his three friends, he gave them such a glare that instinctively they crouched away from the whip, wondering whether he were going to inflict instant punishment upon them. But Christie was only bent on teaching the lesson.

"This is a map," he said. "How many of you have ever seen a map of Florida?"

Several children raised their hands.

"Well, this isn't a map of Florida; it's a map of Palestine, that place that Uncle Moses spoke about when he prayed. And Bethlehem is on it somewhere. See if you can find it anywhere. Because that's the place that the verses that were just read tell about."

Rushforth suddenly roused to helpfulness. He espied Bethlehem, and at the risk of a cut with the whip from the angry Sunday-school superintendent he came forward and put his finger on Bethlehem.

Christie's face cleared. He felt that the waters were not quite so deep, after all. With Bethlehem in sight and Aunt Tildy putting on her spectacles, he felt he had his audience. He turned to the blackboard.

"Now," said he, taking up a piece of yellow chalk, "I'm going to draw a star. That was one of the first Christmas things that happened about that time. While I'm drawing it, I want you to think of some of the other things the lesson tells about; and, if I can, I'll draw them."

The little heads bobbed eagerly this side and that to see the wonder of a star appear on the smooth black surface with those few quick strokes.

"I reckon you bettah put a rainbow up 'bove de stah, fer a promise," put in old Uncle Moses, " 'cause the Scripture say somewhere, 'Where is de promise of His comin'?' An' de rainbow is His promise in de heavens."

"All right," said Christie, breathing more freely, though he did not quite see the connection. And soon a rainbow arch glowed at the top over the star. Then began to grow desire to see this and that ˎ thing drawn, and the scholars, interested beyond their leader's wildest expectations, called out: "Manger, wise men! King!"

Christie stopped at nothing from a sheep to an angel. He made some attempt to draw everything they asked for.

And his audience did not laugh. They were hushed into silence. Part of them were held in thrall by overwhelming admiration for his genius, and the other part by sheer astonishment. The young men, his companions, looked at Christie with a new respect, and gazed gravely from him to a shackly cow, which was intended to represent the oxen that usually fed from the Bethlehem manger, and wondered. A new Christie Bailey was before them, and they knew not what to make of him.

For Christie was getting interested in his work. The blackboard was almost full, and the perspiration was standing out on his brow and making little damp, dark rings of the curls about his forehead.

"There's just room for one more thing. What shall it be, Uncle Moses?" he said as he paused. His face was eager and his voice was interested.

"Better write a cross down, sah, 'cause dat's de reason of dat baby's comin' into dis world. He come to die to save us all."

"Amen!" said Aunt Tildy, wiping her eyes and settling her spectacles for the last picture, and Christie turned with relief back to his almost finished task. A cross was an easy thing to make.

He built it of stone, massive and strong; and, as its arms grew, stretched out to save, something of its grandeur and purpose seemed to enter his mind and stay.

"Now let's sing 'Rock of Ages,'" said Uncle Moses, closing his eyes with a happy smile, and the choir hastily found it and began.

As the Sunday school rose to depart, and shuffled out with many a scrape and bow and admiring glance backward at the glowing blackboard, Christie felt a hand touch his arm; and, glancing down, he saw a small girl with great, dark eyes set in black fringes gazing up at the picture above the organ, her little bony hand on his sleeve.

"Is dat man yoh all's fader?" she asked him, timidly.

A great wave of color stole up into Christie's face.

"No," he answered. "That is a picture of Jesus when He grew up to be a man."

"O!" gasped the little girl, in admiration, "did you done draw dat? Did you all evah see Jesus?"

The color deepened.

"No, I did not draw that picture," said Christie; "it was sent a present to me."

"O," said the child, disappointed, "I thought you'd maybe seed Him sometime. But He look like you, He do. I thought He was you all's fader."

The little girl turned away, but her words lingered in Christie's heart. His Father! How that stirred some memory! His Father in heaven! Had he perhaps spoken wrong when he claimed no relationship with Jesus, the Christ?

Chapter 6

"My Father!"

The three young men who had come to play a practical joke had stayed to clear up. Gravely and courteously they had gone about the work, had piled the hymn-books neatly on the top of the organ, and placed the boards and boxes away under the house for further use if needed, for the entire Sunday school had declared, upon leaving the house with a bow and a smile, "I'll come again next Sunday, Mistah Christie,; I'll come *every* Sunday." And Christie had not said them nay.

The young men had bade a quiet good evening to their host, not once calling him "Miss Christie," had voted the afternoon a genuine success, and were actually gone.

Christie sank to the couch, and looked into the eyes looking down upon him.

He was tired. O, he was more tired than he had ever been in his life before! He was so tired he would like to cry. And the pictured eyes seemed yearning to comfort him.

He thought of the words of the little black girl. "Is dat man you's fader?"

"My Father!" he said aloud. "My Father!" The words echoed with a pleasant ring in the little silent, lonely room. He did not know why he said it, but he repeated it again.

And now if the traditions of his childhood had been filled with the Bible, a host of verses would have flocked about him; but, as his mind had not been filled with holy things, he had it all to learn, and his ideas of the Man, Christ Jesus, were of the vaguest and crudest. And perhaps, as to the children of old, God was speaking directly to his heart.

61

Christie lay still and thought. Went over all his useless life, and hated it; went over the past week with its surprises, and then over the strange afternoon. His own conduct seemed to him the most surprising, after all. Now why, just *why,* had he thrown that case of liquor out of the door, and why had he gone ahead with that Sunday school? There was a mysterious power at work within him. Was the secret the presence of the Man of the picture?

The sun dropped over the rim of the flat, low horizon, and left the pines looming dark against a starry sky. All the earth went dark with night. And Christie lay there in the quiet darkness, yet not alone. He kept thinking over what the little girl had said to him, and once again he said it out loud in the hush of the room, "My Father!"

But, as the darkness grew deeper, there seemed to be a luminous halo up where he knew the picture hung, and while he rested there with closed eyes he felt that presence growing brighter. Those kind eyes were looking down upon him out of the dark of the room.

This time he called, "My Father!" with recognition in his voice, and out from the shadows of his life the Christ stepped nearer till He stood beside the couch, and, stooping, blessed him, breathed His love upon him, while he looked up in wonder and joy. And, perhaps because he was not familiar with the words of Christ, the young man was unable to recall in what form those precious words of blessing had fallen upon his ear during the dream, or trance, or whatever it might be, that had come upon him.

When the morning broke about him, Christie, waking, sat up and remembered, and decided that it must have been a dream induced by the unusual excitement of the day before; yet there lingered with him a wondrous joy for which he could not account.

Again and again he looked at the picture reverently, and said under his breath, "My Father."

He began to wonder whether he was growing daft. Perhaps his long loneliness was enfeebling his mind that he was so susceptible to what he had always considered superstition; nevertheless, it gave him joy, and he finally decided to humor himself in this fancy. This was the permission of his old self toward the new self that was being born within him.

He went about his work singing,

"He holds the key of all unknown,
And I am glad—"

"Well, I *am* glad!" he announced aloud, as if some one had disputed the fact he had just stated. "About the safest person to hold the key, after all, I guess;" and even as a maiden might steal a glance to the eyes of her lover, so the soul in him glanced up to the eyes of the picture.

The dog and the pony rejoiced as they heard their master's cheery whistle, and Christie felt happier that day than he had since he was a little boy.

Towards night he grew quieter. He was revolving a scheme. It would be rather interesting to write out an account of the Sunday school, not, of course, the part the fellows had in it, for that must not be known, but just the pleasant part, about Uncle Moses and Aunt Tildy. He would write it to Hazel Winship,—not that it was likely he would ever send it, but it would be pleasant work to pretend to himself he was writing her another letter. He had not enjoyed anything for a long time as much as he enjoyed writing that letter to her the other day.

Perhaps after a long time, if she ever answered his letter,—and here he suddenly realized that he was cherishing a faint hope in his heart that she would answer it,—he might revise this letter and send it to her. It would please her to know he was trying to do his best with a Sunday school for her, and she would be likely to appreciate some of the things that had happened. He would do it; he would do it this very evening.

He hurried through his day's work with a zest. There was something to look forward to in the evening. It was foolish, perhaps, but surely no more foolish than his amusements the last four years had been. It was innocent, at least, and could do no one any harm.

Then, as he sat down to write, he glanced instinctively to the picture. It still wove its spell of the eyes about him, and he had not lost the feeling that Christ had come to him, though he had never made the slightest attempt or desired to come to Christ. And under the new influence he wrote his thoughts, as one might wing a prayer, scarce believing it would ever reach a listening ear, yet taking comfort in the sending. And so he wrote:

* * *

"*My dear new Friend:*—I did not expect to write to you again; at least, not so soon; for it seems impossible that one so blessed with this world's good things should have time to care to think twice of one like me. I do not even know now whether I shall ever send this when it is written, but it will while away my lonely evening to write, and give me the pleasure of a little talk with a companion whom I much appreciate, and if I never send it, it can do no harm.

"It is about the Sunday school. You know I told you I could never do anything like that; I did not know how; and I never dreamed that I could—or would, perhaps I ought to say—more than to give the negroes the papers you sent and let them hear the organ sometimes. But a very strange thing has happened. A Sunday school has come to me in spite of myself.

"The friend who was playing the organ this Christmas morning, when the black children stood at the door listening, in jest invited them to a Sunday school, and they came. I was vexed because I did not know what to do with them. Then, too, the friend came, bringing two others; and they all thought it was a huge joke. I saw they were going to act out a farce; and, while I never had much conscience about these things before, I seemed to know that it would not be what you would like. Then, too, that wonderful picture that you sent disturbed me. I did not like a laugh at religion with that picture looking on.

"You may perhaps wonder at me. I do not understand myself, but that picture has had a strange effect upon me. It made me do a lot of things Sunday that I did not want to do. It made me take hold and do something to make that Sunday school go right. I didn't know how in the least. Of course I've been to Sunday school; I did not mean that; but I never took much notice of things, how they were done; and I was not one to do it, anyway. I felt my unfitness dreadfully, and all the more because those friends of mine were here, and I knew they were making fun. I made them sing a lot, and then I asked old Uncle Moses to help us out. I wish I could show you Uncle Moses."

Here the writer paused, and seemed to be debating a point a moment, and then rapidly wrote:

"I'll try to sketch him roughly."

There followed a spirited sketch of Uncle Moses with both hands crossed atop his heavy cane, his benign chin leaning forward interestedly. One could fairly see how yellow with age were his whitened locks, how green with age his ancient coat. Christie had his talents, though there were few outlets for them.

It is of interest to note just here that, when this letter reached the Northern college, as it did one day, those six girls clubbed together, and laughed and cried over the pictures, and finally, after due council, Christie Bailey was offered a full course in a famous woman's college of art. This he smiled over and quietly declined, saying he was much too old to begin anything like that, which required that one should begin at babyhood to accomplish anything by it. This the girls sighed over and argued over, but finally gave up, as they found Christie wouldn't.

But to return to the letter. Christie gave a full account of the prayer, which had touched his own heart deeply. Then he described and sketched Aunt Tildy with her spectacles. He had a secret longing to put in Armstrong with his glasses and the incident of his interruption with the Bible-reading; but, as that would reflect somewhat upon his character as an elderly maiden, to be found consorting with three such young men, he restrained himself. But he put an extra vigor into the front row of little black heads, bobbing this way and that, singing with might and main.

"I knew they ought to have a lesson next, but I didn't know how to teach it any better than I know how to make an orange-tree bear in a hurry. However, I determined to do my best. I happened to remember there had been something said in what was read about a star; so I made one, and told them each to think of something they had heard about in that lesson that they wanted me to draw. That worked first-rate. They tried everything, pretty near, in the encyclopædia, and I did my best at each till the whole big blackboard was full. I wish you could see it. It looks like a Noah's ark hanging up there on the wall now, for I have not cleaned it off yet. I keep it there to remind me that I really did teach a Sunday-school class once.

"When they went away, they all said they were coming again, and I don't doubt they'll do it. I'm sure I don't know what to do with them if they do, for I've drawn all there is to draw; and, as for teaching them anything, they can teach me more in a minute than I could teach them in a century. Why, one little child looked up at me with her big, round, soft eyes, for all the world like my faithful dog's eyes, so wistful and pretty, and asked me if that picture on the wall was my father.

"I wish I knew more about that picture. I know it must be meant for Jesus Christ. I am not quite so ignorant of all religion as not to see that. There is the halo with the shadow of the cross above His head. And, when the sun has almost set, it touches there, and the halo seems to glow and glow almost with phosphorescent light until the sun is gone and leaves us all in darkness; and then I fancy I can see it yet glow out between the three arms of the cross.

"And now I do not know why I am writing this. I did not mean to do so when I began, but I feel as if I must tell of the strange experience I had last night."

And then Christie told his dream. Told it till one reading could but feel as he felt, see the vision with him, yearn for the blessing, and be glad and wonder always after.

"Tell me what it means," he wrote. "It seems as if there was something in this presence for me. I cannot believe that it is all imagination, for it would leave me when day comes. It has set me longing for something, I know not what. I never longed before, except for my oranges to bring me money. When I wanted something I could not have, heretofore, I went and did something I knew I ought not, just for pleasure of doing wrong, a sort of defiant pleasure. Now I feel as if I wanted to do right, to be good, like a little child coming to its father. I feel as if I wanted to ask you, as that little soul asked me yesterday, 'Do you all's know that Man?' "

Christie folded his letter, and flung it down upon the table with his head upon his hands. With the writing of that experience the strength seemed to have gone out of him. He felt abashed in its presence. He seemed to have avowed something, to have made a declaration of desire and intention for which he was hardly ready yet; and still he did not want to go back. He was like a man groping in the dark, not knowing where he was, or whether there was light, or whether indeed he wanted the light if there was any to be had.

But before he retired that night he dropped upon his knees beside his couch, with bowed and reverent head, and after waiting silently awhile he said aloud, "My Father!" as if he were testing a call. He repeated it again, more eagerly, and a third time, with a ring in his voice, "My Father!"

That was all. He did not know how to pray. His soul had grown no farther than just to know how to call to his Father, but it was enough. A kind of peace seemed to settle down upon him, a feeling that he had been heard.

Once more there came to him a knowledge that he was acting out of all reason, and he wondered whether he could be losing his mind. He, a red-haired, hard-featured orange-grower, who but yesterday had carried curses so easily upon his lips, and might again to-morrow, to be allowing his emotions thus to carry him away! It was simply childish!

But so deep was the feeling that a Friend was near, that he might really say, "My Father," if only to the dark, that he determined to keep up the hallucination, if indeed hallucination it was, as long as it would last. And so he fell asleep again to dream of benediction.

And on the morrow a sudden desire took him to mail that letter he had written the night before. And what harm, since he would never see the girl, and since she thought him a poor, forlorn creature—half daft this letter might prove him; but even so she might write him again, which result he found he wanted very much when he came to think about it; and so without giving himself a chance to repent by rereading it he drove the limping pony to town and mailed it.

Now, as it came on toward the middle of the week, a conviction suddenly seized Superintendent Christie Bailey that another Sunday was about to dawn and another time of trial would perhaps be his. He had virtually bound himself to that Sunday school by the mailing of that foolish letter. He could have run away if it had not been for that, and those girls up North would never have bothered their heads any more about their old Sunday school. What if Mortimer should bring the fellows over from the lake? What if! Oh, horror! His blood froze in his veins.

Chapter 7

"I Love You"

After his supper that night he doggedly seized the lesson leaf, and began to study. He read the whole thing through, hints and suggestions and elucidations and illustrations and all, and then began over again.

At last it struck him that the hints for the infant class would about suit his needs, and without further ado he set himself to master them. Before long he was interested as a child in his plans, and the next evening was spent in cutting out paper crosses as suggested in the lesson, one for every scholar he expected to be present, and lettering them with the golden text.

He spent another evening still in making an elaborate picture on the reverse side of the blackboard, to be used at the close of his lesson after he had led up to it by more simple work on the other side.

He even went so far as to take the hymn-book and select the hymns, and to write out a regular programme. No one should catch him napping this time. Neither should the prayer be forgotten. Uncle Moses would be there, and they could trust him to pray.

Christie was a little anxious about his music, for upon that he depended principally for success. He felt surprised over himself that he so much wished to succeed, when a week ago he had not cared. What would he do, though, if Mortimer did not turn up, or, worse still, if he had planned more mischief?

But the three friends appeared promptly on the hour, gravity on their faces and helpfulness in the very atmosphere that surrounded them. They had no more practical jokes to play. They had recognized that for some hidden reason Christie meant to play this thing out in earnest, and their liking and respect for him were such that they wanted to assist in the same spirit.

71

They liked him none the less for his prompt handling of the case of liquors. They carried a code of honor in that colony that respected moral courage when they saw it. Besides, everybody liked Christie.

They listened gravely to Christie's lesson, even with interest. They took their little paper crosses, and studied them curiously, and folded them away in their breast pockets,—Armstrong had passed them about, being careful to reserve three for himself, Mortimer, and Rushforth,—and they sang with a right good will.

And, when the time came to leave, they shook hands with Christie like the rest, and without the least mocking in their voices said they had had a pleasant time and they would come again. Then each man took up a box and a board, and stowed them away as he passed out.

And thus was Christie set up above the rest to a position of honor and respect. This work that he had taken up—that they had partly forced him to take up—separated him from them somewhat, and perhaps it was this fact that Christie had to thank afterward for his freedom from temptation during those first few weeks of the young man's acquaintance with his heavenly Father.

For how would it have been possible for him to grow into the life of Christ if he had been constantly meeting and drinking liquor with these boon companions?

The new life could not have grown with the old.

Christie's action that first Sunday afternoon had made a difference between him and the rest. They could but recognize it, and they admired it in him; therefore they set him up. What was there for Christie but to try to act up to his position?

Before the end of another week there arrived from the North a package of books and papers and Sunday-school cards and helps such as would have delighted the heart of the most advanced Sunday-school teacher of the day. What those girls could not think of, the head of the large religious bookstore to which they had gone thought of for them, and Christie had food for thought and action during many a long, lonely evening.

And always these evenings ended in his kneeling in the dark, where he fancied the light of Christ's halo in the picture could send its glow upon him, and saying aloud in a clear voice, "My Father," while outside in the summer-winter night was only the wailing of the tall pines as they waved weird fingers dripping with gray moss, or the plaintive call of the tit-wil-low, through the night.

There had come with the package, too, a letter for Christie. He put it in his breast pocket with glad anticipation, and hustled that pony home at a most unmerciful trot; at least, so thought the pony.

When Hazel Winship read that second letter aloud to the other girls, she did not read the whole of it. The pages which contained the sketches she passed around freely, and they read and laughed over the Sunday school, and talked enthusiastically of its future; but the pages which told of the Sabbath-evening vision and of Christie's feeling toward the picture Hazel kept to herself.

She felt instinctively that Christie would rather not have it shown. It seemed so sacred to her and so wonderful. Her heart went out to the other soul seeking its Father.

When they were all gone out of her room that night, she locked her door and knelt a long time praying, praying for the soul of Christie Bailey. Something in the longing of that letter from the South had reproached her, that she, with all her helps to enlightenment, was not appreciating to its full the love and care of her heavenly Father. And so Christie unknowingly helped Hazel Winship nearer to her Master.

And then Hazel wrote the letter, in spite of a Greek thesis, THE thesis in fact, that was waiting and calling to her with urgency—the letter that Christie carried home in his breast pocket.

He did not wait to eat his supper, though he gave the pony his. Indeed, it was not a very attractive function at its best.

Christie was really handsome that night, with the lamplight bringing out all the copper tints and garnet shadows in his hair. His finely cut lips curled in a pleasant smile of anticipation. He had not realized before how much, how very much, he wanted to hear from Hazel Winship again.

His heart was thumping like a girl's as he tore open the delicately perfumed envelope and took out the many closely written pages of the letter; and his heart rejoiced that it was long and closely written. He resolved to read it slowly and make it last a good while.

"My dear, dear Christie," it began, "your second letter has come, and first I want to tell you that I *love* you."

Christie gasped, and dropped the sheets upon the table, his arms and face upon him. His heart was throbbing painfully, and his breath felt like great sobs.

When he raised his eyes by and by, as he was growing to have a habit of doing, to the picture, they were full of tears; and they fell and blurred the delicate writing of the pages on the table, and the Christ knew and pitied him, and seemed almost to smile.

No one had ever told Christie Bailey of loving him, not since his mother those long years ago had held him to her breast and whispered to God to make her little Chris a good man.

He had grown up without expecting love. He scarcely thought he knew the meaning of the word. He scorned it in the only sense he ever heard it spoken of. And now, in all his loneliness, when he had almost ceased to care what the world gave him, to have this free, sweet love of a pure-hearted girl rushed upon him without stint and without cause overpowered him.

Of course he knew it was not his, this love she gave so freely and so frankly. It was meant for a person who never existed, a nice, homely old maid, whose throne in Hazel's imagination had come to be located in his cabin for some strange, wonderful reason; but yet it was his, too, his to enjoy, for it certainly belonged to no one else. He was robbing no one else to let his hungry heart be filled a little while with the fulness of it.

One resolve he made instantly, without hesitation, and that was that he would be worthy of such love if so be it in him lay to be. He would cherish it as a tender flower that had been meant for another, but had fallen instead into his rough keeping; and no thought or word or action of his should ever stain it.

Then with true knighthood in his heart to help him onward he raised his head and read on, a great joy upon him which almost ingulfed him.

"And I believe you love me a little, too."

Christie caught his breath again. He saw that it was true, although he had not known it before.

"Shall I tell you why I think so? Because you have written me this little piece out of your heart-life, this story of your vision of Jesus Christ, for I believe it was such.

"I have not read that part of your letter to the other girls. I could not. It seemed sacred; and, while I know they would have sympathized and understood, yet I felt perhaps you wrote it just to me, and I would keep it sacred for you.

"And so I am sending you this little letter just to speak of that to you. I shall write in my other letter with the rest of the girls, all about the Sunday school, how glad we are, and all about the pictures how fine they are; and you will understand. But this letter is all about your own self.

"I have stopped most urgent work upon my thesis to write this, too; so you may know how important I consider you, Christie. I could not sleep last night, for praying about you."

It was a wonderful revelation to Christie, that story of the longing of another soul that his might be saved. To the lonely young fellow, grown used as he was to thinking that not another one in all the world cared for him, it seemed almost unbelievable.

He forgot for the time that she considered him another girl like herself. He forgot everything save her pleading that he would give himself to Jesus. She wrote of Jesus Christ as one would write of a much-loved friend, met often face to face, consulted about everything in life, and trusted beyond all others.

A few weeks ago this would indeed have been wonderful to the young man, but that it could have any relation to himself—impossible! Now, with the remembrance of his dream, and the joy his heart had felt from the presence of a picture in his room, it seemed it might be true that Christ would love even him, and with so great a love.

The pleading took hold upon him. Jesus was real to this one girl; He might become real to him.

The thought of that girlish figure kneeling beside her bed in the solemn night hours praying for him was almost more than he could bear. It filled him with awe and a great joy. He drew his breath in sobs, and did not try to keep the tears from flowing. It seemed that the fountains of the years were broken up in him, and he was weeping out his cry for the lonely, unloved childhood he had lost, and the bitter years of mistakes that had followed.

It appeared that the Bible had a great part to play in this new life put before him. Verses which he recognized as from the Scripture abounded in the letter, which he did not remember ever to have heard before, but which came to him with a rich sweetness as if spoken just for him.

Did the Bible contain all that? And why had he not known it before? He had gone to other books for respite from his loneliness. Why had he never known that here was deeper comfort than all else could give?

"Think of it, Christie," the letter said; "Jesus Christ would have come to this earth and lived and died to save you if you had been the only one out of the whole earth that was going to accept Him."

He turned his longing eyes to the picture. Was that true? And the eyes seemed to answer, "Yes, Christie, I would."

Before he turned out his light that night he took the Bible from the organ, and, opening at random, read, "For I have loved thee with an everlasting love; therefore with loving-kindness have I drawn thee." And a light of belief overspread his face. He could not sleep for many hours, for thinking of it all.

There was no question in his mind of whether he would or not. He felt he was the Lord's in spite of everything else. The loving-kindness that had drawn him had been too great for any human resistance.

Then with the realization of the loving-kindness had come self-reproach for his so long denial and worse than indifference. He did not understand the meaning of repentance and faith, but he was learning them in his life.

Christie was never the same after that night. Something had changed in him. It may have been growing all those days since the things first came, but that letter from Hazel Winship marked a decided epoch in his life. All his manhood rose to meet the sweetness of the girl's unasked prayer for him.

It mattered not that she thought not of him as a man. She had prayed, and the prayer had reached up to heaven and back to him again.

The only touch of sadness about it was that he should never be able to see her and thank her face to face for the good she had done to him. He thought of her as some far-away angel who had stooped to earth for a little while, and in some of his reveries dreamed that perhaps in heaven, where all things are made right, he should know her. For the present it was enough that he had her sweet friendship, and her companionship in writing.

Not for worlds now would he reveal his identity. And the thought that this might be wrong did not enter his mind. What harm could it possibly do? and what infinite good to himself!—and perhaps through himself to a few of those little black children. He let this thought come timidly to the front.

This was the beginning of the friendship that made life a new thing to Christie Bailey. Long letters he wrote, telling the thoughts of his inmost heart as he had never told them to any one on earth, as he would never have been able to tell them to one whom he hoped to meet sometime, as he would have told them to God.

And the college student found time amid her essays and her fraternities to answer them promptly.

Her companions wondered why she wasted so much valuable time on that poor "cracker" girl, as they sometimes spoke of Christie, and how she could have patience to write so long letters; but their curiosity did not go so far as to wonder what she found to say; else they might have noticed that less and less often did Hazel offer to read aloud her letters from the Southland. But they were busy, and only occasionally inquired about Christie now, or sent a message.

Hazel herself sometimes wondered why this stranger girl had taken so deep a hold upon her; but the days went by and the letters came frequently, and she never found herself willing to put one by unanswered. There was always some question that needed answering, some point on which her young convert to Jesus Christ needed enlightenment.

Then, too, she found herself growing nearer to Jesus because of this friendship with one who was just learning to trust Him in so childlike and earnest a way.

"Do you know," she said confidingly to Ruth Summers one day, "I cannot make myself see Christie Bailey as homely? It doesn't seem possible to me. I think she is mistaken. I know I shall find something handsome about her when I see her, which I shall some day."

And Ruth smiled mockingly. "O Hazel, Hazel, it will be better, then, for you never to see poor Christie, I am sure; for you will surely find your ideal different from the reality."

But Hazel's eyes grew dreamy, and she shook her head.

"No, Ruth, I'm sure, sure. A girl couldn't have all the beautiful thoughts Christie has, and not be fine in expression. There will be some beauty in her, I am sure. Her eyes, now, I know are magnificent. I wish she would send me a picture; but she won't have one taken, though I've coaxed and coaxed."

Chapter 8

Sad News From the North

In his own heart-life Christie was changing day by day. The picture of Christ was his constant companion. At first shyly and then openly he grew to make a confidant of it. He studied the lines of the face, and fitted them to the lines of the life depicted in the New Testament, and without his knowing it his own face was changing. The lines of recklessness and hardness about his mouth were gone. The dulness of discontent was gone from his eyes. They could light now from within in a flash with a joy that no discouragement could quite quench.

By common consent Christie's companions respected his new way of life, and perhaps after the first few weeks if he had shown a disposition to go back to the old way of doing might have even attempted to keep him to his new course.

They every one knew that their way was a bad way. Each man was glad at heart when Christie made an innovation. They came to the Sunday school and helped, controlling their laughter admirably whenever Uncle Moses gave occasion; and they listened to Christie's lessons, which, to say the least, were original, with a courteous deference, mingled with a kind of pride that one of their number could do this.

They also refrained from urging him to go with them on any more revellings. Always he was asked, but in a tone that he came to feel meant that they did not expect him to accept, and would perhaps have been disappointed if he had done so.

Once, when Christie, unthinkingly, half-assented to go on an all-day's ride with some of them, Mortimer put his hand kindly on Christie's shoulder, and said in a tone Christie had never heard him use before: "I wouldn't, Chris. It might be a bore."

Christie turned, and looked earnestly into his eyes for a minute, and then said, "Thank you, Mort!"

As he stood watching them ride away, a sudden instinct made him reach his hand to Mortimer, and say, "Stay with me this time, old fellow"; but the other shook his head, smiling somewhat sadly, Christie thought, and said as he rode off after the others, "Too late, Chris; it isn't any use."

Christie thought about it a good deal that day as he went about his grove without his customary whistle, and at night, before he began his evening's reading and writing, he knelt and breathed his first prayer for the soul of another.

The winter blossomed into spring, and the soft wind blew the breath of yellow jessamine and bay blossoms from the swamps. Christie's wire fence bloomed out into a mass of Cherokee roses, and among the glossy orange-leaves there gleamed many a white, starry blossom, earnest of the golden fruit to come.

Christie with throbbing heart and shining eyes picked his first orange-blossoms, a goodly handful, and, packing them after the most approved methods for long journeys, sent them to Hazel Winship.

Never any oranges, be they numbered by thousands of boxes, could give him the pleasure that those first white waxen blossoms gave as he laid his face gently among them and breathed a blessing on the one to whom they went, before he packed them tenderly in their box.

Christie was deriving daily joy now from Hazel Winship's friendship. Sometimes when he remembered the tender little sentences in her letters his heart fairly stood still with longing that she might know who he was and yet be ready to say them to him. Then he would crush this wish down, and grind his heel upon it, and tell his better self that only on condition of never thinking such a thought again would he allow another letter written her, another thought sent toward her.

Then would he remember the joy she had already brought into his life, and go smiling about his work, singing,

> "He holds the key of all unknown,
> And I am glad."

Hazel Winship spent that first summer after her graduation, most of it, visiting among her college friends at various summer resorts at seaside or on mountain-top. But she did not forget to cheer Christie's lonely summer days—more lonely now because some of his friends had gone North for a while—with bits of letters written from shady nooks on porch or lawn, or sitting in a hammock.

"Christie, you are my safety-valve," she wrote once. "I think you take the place with me of a diary. Most girls use a diary for that. If I was at home with mother, I might use her sometimes; but there are a good many things that if I should write her she would worry, and there really isn't any need, but I could not make her sure. So you see I have to bother you. For instance, there is a young man here—" Christie drew his brows together fiercely. This was a new aspect. There were other young men, then. Of course—and he drew a deep sigh.

It was during the reading of that letter that Christie began to wish there were some way for him to make his real self known to Hazel Winship. He began to see some reasons why what he had done was not just all right.

But there was a satisfaction in being the safety-valve, and there was delight in their trysting-hour when they met before the throne of God. Hazel had suggested this when she first began to try to help Christie Christward; and they had kept it up, praying for this one and that one and for the Sunday school.

Once Christie had dared to think what joy it would be to kneel beside her and hear her voice praying for him. Would he ever hear her voice? The thought had almost taken his breath away. He had not dared to think of it again.

The summer deepened into autumn; and the oranges, a goodly number for the first crop, green disks unseen amid their background of green leaves, blushed golden day by day. And then, just as Christie was beginning to be hopeful about how much he would get for his fruit, there came a sadness into his life that shadowed all the sunshine, and made the price of oranges a very small affair. For Hazel Winship fell ill.

At first it did not seem to be much—a little indisposition, a headache and loss of appetite. She wrote Christie she did not feel well and could not write a long letter.

Then there came a silence of unusual length, followed by a letter from Ruth Summers, at whose home Hazel had been staying when taken ill. It was brief and hurried, and carried with it a hint of anxiety, which, as the days of silence grew into weeks, made Christie's heart heavy.

"Hazel is very ill indeed," she wrote, "but she has worried so that I promised to write and tell you why she had not answered your letter."

The poor fellow comforted himself day after day with the thought that she had thought of him in all her pain and suffering.

He wrote to Ruth Summers, asking for news of his dear friend; but, whether from the anxiety over the sick one, or from being busy about other things, or it may be from indifference,—he could not tell,—there came no answer for weeks.

During this sad time he ceased to whistle. There grew a sadness in his eyes that told of hidden pain, and his cheery ways with the Sunday school were gone.

One day when his heart had been particularly heavy, and he had found the Sabbath-school lesson almost an impossibility, the little dusky girl who had spoken to him before touched him gently on the arm.

"Mistah Christie feel bad? Is somebody you all love, sick?"

Almost the tears filled Christie's eyes as he looked at her in surprise, and nodded his head.

"Youm 'fraid they die?"

Again Christie nodded. He could not speak; something was choking him. The sympathetic voice of the little girl was breaking down his self-control.

The little black fingers touched his hand sorrowfully, and there was in her eyes a longing to comfort, as she lifted them first to her beloved superintendent's face and then to the picture above them.

"But you all's fathah's not dead," she pleaded, shyly.

Christie caught her meaning in a flash, and marvelled afterwards that a child should have gone so directly to the point, where he, so many years beyond her, had missed it. He had not learned yet how God has revealed the wise things of this world unto the babes.

"No, Sylvie," he said quickly, grasping the timid little fingers; "my Father is not dead. I will take my trouble to Him. Thank you."

The smile that broke over the little girl's face as she said good-night was the first ray of the light that began to shine over Christie Bailey's soul as he realized that God was not dead and God was his Father.

When they were all gone, he locked his doors, and knelt before his heavenly Father, pouring out his anguish, praying for his friend and for himself, yielding up his will, and feeling the return of peace, and surety that God doeth all things well. Again as he slept he saw the vision of the Christ bending over him in benediction, and when he woke he found himself singing softly,

> "He holds the key to all unknown,
> And I am glad."

He wondered whether it was just a happening—and then knew that it was not—that Ruth Summer's second letter reached him that day, saying that Hazel was at last past all danger and had spoken about Christie Bailey, and so she, Ruth, had hastened to send the message on, hoping the far-away friend would forgive her for the delay in answering.

After that Christie believed with his whole soul in prayer.

He set himself the pleasant task of writing to Hazel all he had felt and experienced during her illness and long silence. When she grew well enough to write him again, he might send it. He was not sure.

One paragraph he allowed himself, in which to pour out the pent-up feelings of his heart. But even in this he weighed every word. He began to long to be perfectly true before her, and to wish there were a way to tell her all the truth about himself without losing her friendship. This was the paragraph.

"I did not know until you were silent how much of my life was bound up with yours. I can never tell you how much I love you, but I can tell God about it, the God you taught me to love."

The very next day there came a note from Ruth Summers saying that Hazel was longing to hear from Florida again and that she was now permitted to read her own letters. Then with joy he took his letter to the office, and not long after received a little note in Hazel's own familiar hand, closing with the words: "Who knows? perhaps you will be able to tell me all about it some day, after all." And

Christie, when he read it, held his hand on his heart to still the tumult of pain and joy.

"Have you written to Christie Bailey that you are coming?" said Victoria Landis, turning her eyes from the window of the drawing-room car, where she was studying the changing landscape, so new and strange to her Northern eyes.

"No," said Hazel, leaning back among her pillows; "I thought it would be more fun to surprise her. Besides, I want to see things just exactly as they are, as she has described them to me, you know. I don't want her to go and get fussed up to meet me. She wouldn't be natural at all if she did. I'm positive she's shy, and I must take her unawares. After I have put my arms around her neck in regular girl fashion and kissed her she will realize that it is just I, the one she has written to for a year, and everything will be all right; but if she has a long time to think about it, and conjure up all sorts of nonsense about her dress and mine, and the differences in our stations, she wouldn't be at all the same Christie. I love her just as she is, and that's the way I mean to see her first."

"I am afraid, Hazel, you'll be dreadfully disappointed," said Ruth Summers. "Things on paper are never exactly like the real things. Now look out that window. Is this the land of flowers? Look at all that blackened ground where it's been burnt over, and see those ridiculous green tufts sticking up every little way, varied by a stiff green palm-leaf, as if children had stuck crazy old fans in a play garden. You know the real is never as good as the ideal, Hazel."

"It's a great deal better," said Hazel positively. "Those green tufts, as you call them, are young pines. Some day they'll be magnificent. Those little fans are miniature palms. That's the way they grow down here. Christie has told me all about it. It looks exactly to a dot as I expected, and I'm sure Christie will be even better."

The two travelling companions looked lovingly at her, and remembered how near they had come to losing their friend only a little while before, and said no more to dampen her high spirits. This trip was for Hazel, to bring back the roses to her cheeks; and father, mother, brother, and friends were determined to do all they could to make it a success.

It was the morning after they arrived at the hotel that Hazel asked to be taken at once to see Christie. She wanted to go alone; but, as that was not to be thought of in her convalescent state, she consented to take Ruth and Victoria with her.

"You'll go out in the orange-grove and visit with the chickens while I have a little heart-to-heart talk with Christie, won't you, you dears?" she said, as she gracefully gave up her idea of going alone.

The old man who drove the carriage that took them there was exceedingly talkative. Yes, he knew Christie Bailey; most everybody did. They imparted to him the fact that this visit was to be a surprise party, and arranged with him to leave them for an hour while he went on another errand and returned for them. These matters planned, they settled down to gleeful talk.

Victoria Landis on the front seat with the interested driver—who felt exceedingly curious about this party of pretty girls going to visit Christie Bailey thus secretly—began to question him.

"Is Christie Bailey a very large person?" she asked mischievously. "Is she as large as I am? You see we have never seen her."

The old man looked at her quizzically. "Never seen her? Aw! *O,*" he said dryly. "Wall, yas, fer a *girl,* I should say she *was* ruther *big.* Yas, I should say she was fully as big as you be—if not bigger."

"Has she very red hair?" went on Victoria. There was purpose in her mischief. She did not want Hazel to be too much disappointed.

"Ruther," responded the driver. Then he chuckled unduly, it seemed to Hazel, and added, "Ruther red."

"Isn't she at all pretty?" asked Ruth Summers, leaning forward with a troubled air, as if to snatch one ray of hope.

"Purty!" chuckled the driver. "Wall, no, I shouldn't eggzactly call her purty. She's got nice eyes," he added, as an afterthought.

"There!" said Hazel, sitting up triumphantly. "I knew her eyes were magnificent. Now *please* don't say any more."

The driver turned his twinkly little eyes around, and stared at Hazel, and then clucked the horse over the deep sandy road.

He set them down at Christie's gateway, telling them to knock at the cabin door, and they would be sure to be answered by the owner, and he would return within the hour. Then he drove his horse reluctantly away, turning his head back as far as he could see, hoping Christie would come to the door. He would like to see what happened. For half a mile down the road he laughed to the black-jacks, and occasionally ejaculated: "No, she ain't just to say *purty!* But she's *good.* I might 'a' told 'em she was good."

This was the driver's tribute to Christie.

Chapter 9

The Discovery

Hazel walked up to the door of the cabin in a dream of anticipation realized. Here were the periwinkles nodding their bright eyes along the border of the path, and there the chickens stood on one kid foot of yellow, as Christie had described.

She could almost have found the way here alone, from the letters she had received. She drank in the air, and felt it give new life to her, and thought of the pleasant hours she would spend with Christie during the weeks that were to follow, and of the secret plan she had of taking Christie back home with her for the winter.

They knocked at the door, which was open, and, stepping in, stood surrounded by the familiar things; and all three felt the delight of giving these few simple gifts, which had been so little to them when they were given.

Then a merry whistle sounded from the back yard and heavy steps on the board path at the back door, and Christie walked in from the barn with the frying-pan in one hand and a dish-pan in the other. He had been out to scrape some scraps from his table to the chickens in the yard.

The blood came quickly to his cheeks at sight of his three elegant visitors. He put the cooking-utensils down on the stove with a thud, and drew off his old straw hat, revealing his garnet-tinted hair in all its glory against the sunshine of a Florida sky in the doorway behind him.

"Is Christie Bailey at home?" questioned Victoria Landis, who seemed the natural spokesman for the three.

"*I* am Christie Bailey," said the young man gravely, looking from one to another questioningly. "Won't you sit down?"

There was a moment's pause before the tension broke, and then a pained, sweet voice, the voice of Christie's dreams, spoke forth.

"But Christie Bailey is a young woman."

Christie looked at Hazel, and knew his hour had come.

"No, *I* am Christie Bailey," he said once more, his great, honest eyes pleading for forgiveness.

"Do you really mean it?" said Victoria, amusement growing in her eyes as she noted his every fine point, noted the broad shoulders and the way he had of carrying his head up, noted the flash of his eyes and the toss of rich waves from his forehead.

"And you're not a girl, after all?" questioned Ruth Summers in a frightened tone, looking with troubled eyes from Christie to Hazel, who had turned quite white.

But Christie was looking straight at Hazel, all his soul come to judgment before her, his mouth closed, unable to plead his own cause.

"Evidently not!" remarked Victoria dryly. "What extremely self-evident facts you find to remark upon, Ruth!"

But the others did not hear them. They were facing one another, these two who had held communion of soul for so many months, and who, now that they were face to face, were suddenly cut asunder by an insurmountable wall of a composition known as truth.

Hazel's dark eyes burned wide and deep from her white face. The enthusiasm that could make her love an unseen, unlovely woman, could also glow with the extreme of scorn for one whom she despised. The firm little mouth he had admired was set and stern. Her lips were pallid as her cheeks, while the light of truth and righteousness fairly scintillated from her countenance.

"Then you have been deceiving me all this time!" Her voice was high and clear, tempered by her late illness, and keen with pain. Her whole alert, graceful body expressed the utmost scorn. She would have done for a model of the figure of Retribution.

And yet in that awful minute, as Christie met her eye for eye, and saw the judgment of "Guilty" pronounced upon him, and could but acknowledge it just, and saw before him the blankness of the punishment that was to be his, he had time to think with a thrill of delight that Hazel was all and more than he had dreamed of her as being. He had time to be glad that she was as she was. He would not have her changed one whit, retribution and all.

It was all over in a minute; the sentence gone forth, the girl turned and marched with stately step out of the door down the white path to the road. But the little ripples of air she swept by in passing rolled back upon the culprit a knowledge of her disappointment, chagrin, and humiliation.

Christie bowed his head in acceptance of his sentence, and looked at his other two visitors, his eyes beseeching that they would go and leave him to endure what had come upon him. Ruth was clinging to Victoria's arm, frightened. She had seen the delicate white of Hazel's cheek as she went out the door. But Victoria's eyes were dancing with fun.

"Why didn't you *say* something?" she demanded of Christie. "Go out and stop her before she gets away! See, she is out there by the hedge. You can make it all right with her." There was pity in her voice. She liked the honest eyes and fine bearing of the young man. Besides, she loved fun, and did not like to see this most enticing situation spoiled at the climax.

A light of hope sprang into Christie's eyes as he turned to follow her suggestion. It did not take him long to overtake Hazel's slow step in the deep, sandy way.

"I must tell you how sorry I am—" he began before he had quite caught up to her.

But she turned and faced him with her hand lifted in protest.

"If you are sorry, then please do not say another word. I will forgive you, of course, because I am a Christian; but don't ever speak to me again. I HATE deceit!" Then she turned and sped down the road like a flash, in spite of her weakness.

And Christie stood in the road where she left him, his head bared to the winter's sunshine, looking as if he had been struck in the face by a loved hand, his whole strong body trembling.

Victoria meanwhile was taking in the situation. She espied Hazel's photograph framed in a delicate tracery of Florida moss. Then she frowned. Hazel would never permit that to stay here now, and her instinct told her that it would be missed by its present owner, and that he had the kind of honor that would not keep it if it were demanded.

"This must not be in sight when Hazel comes back," she whispered softly, disengaging herself from Ruth's clinging hand, and going vigorously to work. She took down the photograph, slipped off the moss, and, looking about for a place of concealment, hid it in the breast pocket of an old coat lying on a chair near by. Then, going to the door, she watched for developments; but, as she perceived that Hazel had fled and Christie was dazed, she made up her mind that she was needed elsewhere, and, calling Ruth, hurried down the road.

"If you miss anything, look in your coat pocket for it," she said as she passed Christie in the road. But Christie was too much overcome to take in what she meant.

He went back to his cabin. The light of the world seemed crushed out for him. Even the organ and the couch and the various pretty touches that had entered his home through these Northern friends of a year ago seemed suddenly to have withdrawn themselves from him, as if they had discovered the mistake in his identity, and were frowning their disapproval and letting him know that he was holding property under false pretences. Only the loving eyes of the pictured Christ looked tenderly at him, and with a leap of his heart Christie realized that Hazel had given him one thing that she could never take away.

With something almost like a sob he threw himself on his knees before the picture and cried out in anguish, "My Father!"

Christie did not get supper that night. He forgot that there was any need for anything but comfort and forgiveness in the world. He knelt there, praying, sometimes, but most of the time just letting his heart lie bleeding and open before his Father's eyes.

The night came on, and still he knelt.

By and by there came a kind of comfort in remembering the little black girl's words, "You all's Fathah's not dead." He was not cut off from his Father. Something like peace settled upon him, a resignation and a strength to bear.

To think the situation over clearly and see whether there was aught he could do was beyond him. His rebuke had come. He could not justify himself. He had done wrong, though without intention. Beside, it was too late to do anything now. He had been turned out of Eden. The angel with the flaming sword had bidden him no more think to enter. He must go forth and labor, but God was not dead.

The days after that passed slowly and dully. Christie hardly took account of time. He was like one laden with a heavy burden and made to draw it on a long road. He had started, and was plodding his best every day, knowing that there would be an end sometime; but it was to be hard and long.

Gradually he came out of the daze that Hazel's words had put upon him. Gradually he felt himself forgiven by God for his deceit. But he would not discuss even with his own heart the possibility of forgiveness from Hazel. She was right, of course. He had known from the first that her friendship did not belong to him. He would keep the memory of it safe; and by and by, when he could bear to think it over, it would be a precious treasure. At least, he could prove himself worthy of the year of her friendship he had enjoyed.

But, thinking his sad thoughts and going about the hardest work he could find, he avoided the public road as much as possible, taking to the little by-paths when he went out from his own grove. And thus one morning, emerging from a tangle of hummock land where the live-oaks arched high above him, and the wild grape and jessamine snarled themselves from magnolia to bay-tree in exquisite patterns, and rare orchids defied the world of fashion to find their hidden lofty homes, Christie heard voices near and the soft footfalls of well-shod horses on the rich, rooty earth of the bridle-path.

He stepped to one side to let the riders pass, for the way was narrow. Just where a ray of sunlight came through a clearing he stood, and the light fell all about him, on his bared head, for he held his hat in his hand, making his head look like one from a painting of an old master, all the copper tints shining above the clear depths of his eyes.

He knew who was coming. It was for this he had removed his hat. His forehead shone white in the shadowed road, where the hat had kept off the sunburn; and about his face had come a sadness and a dignity that glorified his plainness.

Hazel rode the forward horse. She looked weary, and the flush in her cheeks was not altogether one of health. She was controlling herself wonderfully, but her strength was not what they had hoped it would be when they brought her to the Southland. The long walk she had taken under pressure of excitement had almost worn her out, and she had been unable to go out since, until this afternoon, when with the sudden wilfulness of the convalescent she had insisted upon a horseback ride. She had gone much further than her two faithful friends had thought wise, and then suddenly turned toward home, too weary to ride rapidly.

And now she came, at this quick turn, upon Christie standing, sun-glorified, his head inclined in deference, his eyes pleading, his whole bearing one of reverence.

She looked at him, and started, and knew him. That was plain. Then, her face a deadly white, her eyes straight ahead, she rode by magnificently, a steady, unknowing gaze that cut him like a knife just glinting by from her in passing.

He bowed his head, acknowledging her right to do thus with him; but all the blood in his body surged into his face, and then, receding, left him as white as the girl who had just passed by him.

Victoria and Ruth, behind, saw and grieved. They bowed graciously to him as if to try to make up for Hazel's act, but he scarcely seemed to see them, for he was gazing down the narrow shadowed way after the straight little figure sitting her horse so resolutely and riding now so fast.

"I did not know you could be so cruel, Hazel," said Victoria, riding forward beside her. "That fellow was just magnificent, and you have stabbed him to the heart."

But Hazel had stopped her horse, dropped her bridle, and was slipping white and limp from her saddle to the ground. She had not heard.

It was Sunday morning before they had time to think or talk more about it. Hazel had made them very anxious. But Sunday morning she felt a little better, and they were able to slip into her darkened room, one at a time, and say a few words to her.

"Something must be done," said Victoria decidedly, scowling out the window at the ripples of the blue lake below the hotel lawn. "I cannot understand how this thing has taken so great a hold upon her. But I feel sure it is that and nothing else that is making her so ill. Don't you feel so, Ruth?"

"It is the disappointment," said Ruth with troubled eyes. "She told me this morning that it almost shook her faith in prayer and God to think that she should have prayed so for the conversion of that girl's soul—"

"And then found out it was a creature, after all, without a soul?" laughed Victoria. She never could refrain from saying something funny whenever she happened to think of it.

But Ruth went on.

"It wasn't his being a man, at all, instead of a girl. She wouldn't have minded who he or she was, if it had not been for the deceit. She says he went through the whole thing with her, professed to be converted and to be a very earnest Christian, and pray for other people, and talked about Christ in a wonderful way—and now to think he did it all for a joke, it just crushes her. She thinks he deceived her of course in those things, too. She says a man who would deceive in one thing would do so in another. She does not believe now even in his Sunday school. And then you know she is so enthusiastic that she must have said a lot of loving things to him. She is just horrified to think she has been carrying on a first-class low-down flirtation with an unknown stranger. I think the sooner she gets away from this country, the better. She ought to forget all about it."

"But she wouldn't forget. You know Hazel. And, besides, the doctor says it might be death to her to go back into the cold now in the present state of her health. No, Ruth, something else has got to be done."

"What can be done, Victoria? You always talk as if *you* could do *any*thing if you only set about it."

"I'm not sure but I could," said Victoria, laughing. "Wait and see. This thing has got to be reduced to plain, commonplace terms, and have all the heroics and tragics taken out of it. I may need your help; so hold yourself in readiness."

After that Victoria went to her room, whence she emerged about an hour later, and took her way by back halls and by-paths, and finally unseen, down the road.

She was not quite sure of her way, but by retracing her steps occasionally she brought up in front of Christie's cabin just as Aunt Tildy was settling her spectacles for the opening hymn.

She reconnoitred a few minutes till the singing was well under way, and then slipped noiselessly through the sand to the side of the house, where after a few experiments she discovered a crevice through which she could get a limited view of the Sunday school.

A smile of satisfaction hovered about her lips. At least, the Sunday school was a fact. So much she learned from her trip. Then she settled herself to listen.

Christie was praying.

It was the first time Christie's voice had been heard by any one but his Master in prayer. It had happened simply enough. Uncle Moses had been sent away to the village for a doctor for a sick child, and there was no one else to pray. To Christie it was not such a trial as it would have been a year ago. He had talked with his heavenly Father many times since that first cry in the night. But he was not an orator. His words were simple.

"Jesus Christ, we make so many mistakes, and we sin so often. Forgive us. We are not worth saving, but we thank Thee that Thou dost love us, even though all the world turn against us, and though we hate our own selves."

Victoria found her eyes filling with tears. If Hazel could but hear that prayer!

Chapter 10

Victoria Has a Finger in the Pie

During the singing of the next hymn the organist came within range of the watcher's eye, and she noted with surprise the young man to whom she had been introduced in the hotel parlor a few evenings before, Mr. Mortimer. He was a cousin of those Mortimers from Boston who roomed next to Ruth. He would be at the hotel again. He would be another link in the evidence. For Victoria had set out to sift the character of Christie Bailey through and through.

She was chained to the spot by her interest during the blackboard lesson, which by shifting her position a trifle she could see as well as hear; but during the singing of the closing hymn she left in a panic, and when the dusky crowd flowed out into the road she was well on her way toward home, and no one save the yellow-footed chickens that had clucked about her feet were the wiser.

Victoria did not immediately make known to Ruth the events of the afternoon. She had other evidence to gather before she presented it before the court. She wanted to be altogether sure of Christie before she put her finger in the pie at all. Therefore she was on the lookout for young Mr. Mortimer.

She had hoped he would visit his aunt Sunday evening, but if he did he was not in evidence. All day Monday she haunted the piazzas and entrances, but he did not come until Tuesday evening.

Victoria in the meanwhile had made herself agreeable to Mrs. Mortimer, and it did not take her long to monopolize the young man when he finally came. Indeed, he had been attracted to her from the first.

They were soon seated comfortably in two large piazza chairs, watching the moon rise out of the little lake and frame itself in wreaths of long gray moss which reached out lace-like fingers and seemed to try to snare it; but always it slipped through until it sailed high above, serene. So great a moon, and so different from a Northern moon!

Victoria had done justice to the scene with a fine supply of adjectives, and then addressed herself to her self-set task.

"Mr. Mortimer, I wonder if you know a man by the name of Bailey down here, Christie Bailey. Tell me about him, please. Who is he, and how did he come by such a queer name? Is it a diminutive of Christopher?"

She settled her fluffy draperies about her in the moonlight, and fastened her fine eyes on Mortimer interestedly; and he felt he had a pleasant task before him to speak of his friend to this charming girl.

"Certainly, I know Chris well. He's one of the best fellows in the world. Yes, his name is an odd one, a family name, I believe, his mother's family name, I think he told me once. No, no Christopher about it, just plain Christie. But how in the world do you happen to know anything about him? He told me once he hadn't a friend left in the North."

Victoria was prepared for this.

"O, I heard some one talking about a Sunday school he had started, and I am interested in Sunday schools myself. Did he come down here as a sort of missionary, do you know?"

She asked the question innocently enough, and Mortimer waxed earnest in his story.

"No, indeed! No missionary about Christie. Why, Miss Landis, a year ago Christie was one of the toughest fellows in Florida. He could play a fine hand at cards, and could drink as much whiskey as the next one; and there wasn't one of us with a readier tongue when it was loosened up with plenty of drinks—"

"I hope you're not one of that kind?" said Victoria, earnestly, looking at the fine, restless eyes and handsome profile outlined in the moonlight.

A shade of sadness crossed his face. No one had spoken to him like that in many a long day. He turned and looked into her eyes earnestly.

"It's kind of you to care, Miss Landis. Perhaps if I had met some one like you a few years ago, I should have been a better fellow." Then he sighed and went on:

"A strange change came over Christie about a year ago. Some one sent him an organ and some fixings for his room, supposing he was a girl—from his name, I believe. They got hold of his name at the freight-station where his goods were shipped. They must have been an uncommon sort of people to send so much to a stranger. There was a fine picture, too, which he keeps on his wall, some religious work of a great artist, I think. He treasures it above his orange-grove, I believe.

"Well, those things made the most marvellous change in that man. You wouldn't have known him. Some of us fellows went to see him soon after it happened, and we thought it would be a joke to carry out the suggestion that had come with the organ that Christie start a Sunday school; so we went and invited neighbors from all round, and went up there Sunday, and fixed seats all over his cabin.

"He was as mad as could be, but he couldn't help himself; so, instead of knocking us all out and sending the audience home, he just pitched in and had a Sunday school. He wouldn't allow any laughing, either. We fellows had taken lunch and a case of bottles over to make the day a success; and, when Armstrong—he's the second son of an earl—came in with the case of liquor, Chris rose in his might. Perhaps you don't know Christie has red hair. Well, he has a temper just like it,—and he suddenly rose up and fairly blazed at us, eyes and hair and face. He looked like a strong avenging angel. I declare, he was magnificent. We never knew he had it in him before.

"Well, from that day forth he took hold of that Sunday school, and he changed all his ways. He didn't go to any more 'gatherings of the clan,' as we called them. We were all so proud of him we wouldn't have let him if he had tried.

"The fellows, some of them, come to the Sunday school and help every Sunday—sing, you know, and play. We all stand by him. He's good as gold. There's not many could live alone in a Florida orange-grove from one year's end to another and keep themselves from evil the way Christie Bailey has. Wouldn't you like to see the Sunday school sometime? I'll get Chris to let me bring you if you say so."

Victoria smilingly said she would enjoy it; and then, her interest in Christie Bailey satisfied, she turned her attention to the young man before her.

"You didn't answer my question a while ago, about yourself." There was pleading in Victoria's voice, and the young man before her was visibly embarrassed. The tones grew more earnest. The moon looked down upon the two sitting there quietly. The voices of the night were all about them, but they heard not. Victoria had found a mission of her own while trying to straighten out another's.

But the next morning early Victoria laid out her campaign. She took Ruth out for a walk, and on the way she told her what she intended to do.

"And you propose to go to Christie Bailey's house this morning, Victoria, without telling Hazel anything about it? Indeed, Vic, I'm not going to do any such thing. What would Mrs. Winship say?"

"Mrs. Winship will say nothing about it, for she will never know anything about it. Besides, I don't care what she says so long as we straighten things out for Hazel. Don't you see Hazel must be made to understand that she hasn't failed, after all, that the young man was in earnest, and really meant to be a Christian, and that the only thing he failed in was in not having courage to speak out and tell her she had made a mistake? He didn't intend any harm, and after it had gone on for a while of course it was all the harder to tell. Now, Ruth, there's no use in your saying you won't go; for I've *got* to have a chaperone, you know; I couldn't go alone, and I *shall* go with or without you; so you may as well come."

Reluctantly Ruth went, half fearful of the result of this daring girl's plan, and only half understanding what it was she meant to do.

Christie came to the door when they knocked. He looked eagerly beyond them into the sunshine, hunting for another face, but none appeared. Victoria's eyes were dancing.

"She isn't here," she said mockingly, rightly interpreting his searching gaze. "So you'd better ask us in, or you won't find out what we came for. It is very warm out here in the sun."

Christie smiled a sad smile, and asked them in. He could not conjecture what they had come for. He stood gravely waiting for them to speak.

"Now, sir," said Victoria with decision, "I want you to understand that you have been the cause of a great deal of suffering and disappointment."

Christie's face took on at once a look of haggard misery as he listened anxiously, not taking his eyes from the speaker's face. Victoria was enjoying her task immensely. The young man looked handsomer with that abject expression on. It would do him no harm to suffer a little longer. Anyway, he deserved it, she thought.

"You were aware, I think, from a letter Miss Summers wrote you, that Miss Winship had been very ill indeed before she came down here—that she almost died."

Here Ruth nodded her head severely. She felt like meting out judgment to this false-hearted young man.

"You do not know perhaps that the long walk she took from your house last week, after the startling revelation she received here, was enough to have killed her in her weak state of health."

Christie's white, anxious face gave Victoria a flitting twinge of conscience as she began to realize that possibly the young man had suffered enough already without anything added by her, but she went on with her prepared programme.

"You probably do not know that, after she had controlled herself the other day when she was riding horseback until she had passed you by, she was utterly overcome by the humiliation of the sight of you, and slipped from her horse in the road, unconscious, since which time she has been hovering between life and death—"

Victoria had carefully weighed that sentence, and decided that, while it might be a trifle overdrawn, the circumstances nevertheless justified the statement, for truly they had held grave fears for Hazel's life several times during the last two or three days.

But a groan escaped the young man's white lips, and Victoria, springing to her feet, realized that his punishment had been enough. She went toward him involuntarily, a glance of pity in her face.

"Don't look like that!" she said. "I think she will get well; but I think, as you're to blame for a good deal of the trouble, it is time you offered to do something."

"What could I do?" said Christie in hoarse eagerness.

"Well, I think perhaps if you were to explain to her how it all happened it might change the situation somewhat."

"She has forbidden me to say a word," answered Christie in white misery.

"O, she has, has she?" said Victoria, surveying him with dissatis-

faction. "Well, you ought to have done it anyway! You should have
insisted! That's a man's part. She's got to know the truth somehow,
and get some of the tragic taken out of this affair, or she will suffer
for it, that's all; and there's no one to explain but you. You see it
isn't the pleasantest thing to find one has written all sorts of confidences to a strange young man. Hazel is blaming herself as any
common flirt might do if she had a conscience. But that, of course,
though extremely humiliating to her pride, isn't the worst. She feels
terribly about your having deceived her and pretending that you
were a Christian, and she all the time praying out her life for you,
while you were having a good joke out of it. It has hurt her self-re-
spect a good deal, but it has hurt her religion more."

Christie raised his head in protest, but Victoria went on.

"Wait a minute, please. I want to tell you that I believe she is mistaken. I don't believe you were playing a part in telling her you had
become a Christian, were you? Or that you were making fun of her
enthusiasm and trying to see how far she would go, just for fun?"

"I have never written anything in joke to Miss Winship. I honor
and respect her beyond any one else on earth. I have never deceived
her in anything except that I did not tell her who I was. I thought
there was no harm in it when I did it, but now I see it was a terrible
mistake. And I feel that I owe my salvation to Miss Winship. She
introduced me to Jesus Christ. I am trying to make Him my guide."

The young man raised his head, and turned his eyes with ac-
knowledgment toward the pictured Christ as he made his declaration of faith. Victoria and Ruth were awed into admiration.

"I almost expected to see a halo spring up behind his aureole of
copper hair," said Victoria to Ruth on the way home.

Victoria had arranged to send him word when he could see
Hazel, and the two girls went away, leaving Christie in a state of
conflicting emotions. He could do nothing. He sat and thought and
thought, going over all his acquaintance with Hazel, singling out
what he had told her of his own feelings toward Christ. And she had
thought he had done it all in joke! He began to see how hideous had
been his action in her eyes. Knowing her pure, lovely soul as he did
through her letters, he felt keenly for her. How could he blame her
for her saintly condemning of him? And it was that day that he
found in the breast pocket of his old working-coat the photograph

of Hazel so much prized and so sadly missed since the day of her visit. He had supposed Victoria took it, but now he recalled her words about it as she ran after Hazel; and, smiling into the sweet, girlish face, he wondered whether she would ever forgive him.

The next day there came a note from Victoria, saying he might call at seven o'clock on Saturday evening, and Hazel would likely be able to see him a few minutes. A postscript in the writer's original style added: "And I *hope* you'll have sense enough to know what to say! If you don't, I'm sure I can't do anything more for you."

And Christie echoed the cry too deeply to be able to smile over it.

Victoria had laid her plans carefully. She arranged to spend more time with Hazel than she had been doing, pleading a headache as an excuse from going out for a ride in the hot sun, and sending Mrs. Winship in her place more than once. She found that Hazel had no intention of opening her heart to her; so she determined to make a move herself.

Hazel had been very quiet for a long time. Victoria thought she was asleep until at last she noticed a little quiver of her lip and the tiniest glisten of a tear rolling down the thin white cheek.

Without seeming to see she got up and moved around the room a moment, and then in a cheery tone began to tell her story.

"Hazel, dear, I'm going to tell you where I went last Sunday. It was so interesting! I wandered off alone out into the country, and by and by I heard some singing in a little log cabin by the road, and I slipped into the yard behind some crape myrtle bushes all in lovely bloom, where I was entirely hidden.

"I looked through a crack between the logs, and there I saw three rows of black children, and some older people, too, and at the organ—for there was a nice organ standing against the wall—sat Mr. Mortimer, that young man we met in the parlor the other evening, Mrs. Boston Mortimer's nephew, you know. There were some other white young men, too; and they were all singing.

"And after the singing there was a prayer. One of the young men prayed. It was all about being forgiven for mistakes and sins, and not being worth Christ's saving. It was a beautiful prayer! And, Hazel, it was Christie Bailey who prayed!"

Chapter 11

A Daring Manœuvre

Hazel caught her breath, when she heard of Christie's prayer, and a bright flush glowed on her cheek; but Victoria went on:

"Then he taught the lesson, and he did it well. Those little children never stirred, they were so interested; and just as they were singing the closing hymn I came away in a hurry so they would not see me."

Victoria had timed her story from the window. She knew the carriage had returned and that Mother Winship would soon appear at the doorway. There would be no chance for Hazel to speak until she thought about the Sunday school a little while. The footsteps were coming along the hall now, and she could hear Ruth calling to Hazel's brother. She had one more thing to say. She came quite near to the couch, and whispered in Hazel's ear:

"Hazel, I don't believe he has deceived you about everything. I believe you have done him a great deal of good. Don't fret about it, dear."

Hazel was brighter that evening, and often Victoria caught her looking thoughtfully at her. The next day when they were left alone she said, "Tell me what sort of lesson they had at the Sunday school, Vic, dear."

And Victoria launched into a full account of the blackboard lesson and the queer-shaped little cards, which she could not quite see through the crack, that were passed around at the close, and treasured, she could see. Then cautiously she told of the interview with Mr. Mortimer and his account of Christie's throwing the bottles out the door. The story lost none of its color from Victoria's repetition of it; and, when she finished, Hazel's eyes were bright and she was sitting up and smiling.

111

"Wasn't that splendid, Vic?" she said, and then remembered and sank back thoughtfully upon the couch.

Victoria was glad the others came in just then and she could slip away. She had said all she wished to say at present, and would let things rest now until Saturday evening when Christie came.

Victoria had arranged with Mrs. Winship to stay up-stairs and have dinner with Hazel on Saturday evening while the family with Ruth Summers went down to the dining-room. She also arranged with the head waiter to send up Hazel's dinner early. And so by dint of much manœuvring the coast was clear at seven, Hazel's dinner and her own disposed of, and the family just gone down to the dining-room, where they would be safe for at least an hour.

It was no part of Victoria's plan that Mother Winship or Tom or the Judge should come in at an inopportune moment and complicate affairs until Hazel had had everything fully explained to her. After that Victoria felt that she would wash her hands of the whole thing.

Mother Winship had just rustled down the hall, and Victoria, who had been standing by the hall door, waiting until she should be gone, came over to where Hazel sat in a great soft chair by an open fire of pine-knots.

"Hazel," she said in her matter-of-fact, everyday tone, "Christie Bailey has come to know if he may see you for a few minutes. He wants to say a few words of explanation to you. He has really suffered very much, and perhaps you will feel less humiliated by this whole thing if you let him explain. Do you feel able to see him now?"

Hazel looked up, a bright flush on her cheeks.

Victoria betrayed by not so much as the wavering of an eyelash that she was anxious as to the outcome of this simple proposal. Hazel's clear eyes searched her face, and she bore the scrutiny well.

Then Hazel sighed a troubled little breath, and said: "Yes, I will see him, Vic. I feel quite strong to-night, and—I guess it will be better, after all, for me to see him."

Then Victoria felt sure that it was a relief to have him come, and that Hazel had been longing for it for several days.

Christie came in gravely with the tread of one who entered a sacred place, and yet with the quiet dignity of a "gentleman unafraid." Indeed, so far had the object of his visit dominated him that he forgot to shrink from contact with the fashionable world from which he had been so entirely shut away for so long.

He was going to see Hazel. It was the opportunity of his life. As to what came after, it mattered not, now that the great privilege of entering her presence had been accorded him. He had not permitted himself to believe that she would see him even after he had sent up his card, as directed, to Miss Landis.

Victoria shut the door gently behind him, and left them together. She had prepared a chair not far away, where she might sit and guard the door against intrusion; and so she sat and listened to the far-away hum of voices in the dining-room, the tinkle of silver and glass, and the occasional burst from the orchestra in the balcony above the dining-room. But her heart stood still outside the closed door, and wondered whether she had done well or ill, and feared—now that she had done it—all evil things that can pass in review at such a time for judgment on one's own deeds.

Christie stood still before Hazel. The sight of her so thin and white, changed even from a week ago, startled him,—condemned him again, took away his power of speech for the moment.

She was all in soft white cashmere draperies, with delicate lace that fell over the little white wrists as petals of a flower. Her soft brown hair made a halo for her face, and was drawn simply and carelessly together at the back. Christie had never seen any one half so lovely. He caught his breath in admiration of her. He stood and did her reverence.

For one long minute they looked at each other, and then Hazel, who felt it hers to speak first, as she had silenced him before, said, as a young queen might have said, with just the shadow of a smile flickering over her face, "You may sit down."

The gracious permission, accompanied by a slight indication of the chair facing her own by the fire, broke the spell that bound Christie's tongue, and with a heart beating high over what he had come to say he began.

And the words he spoke were not the carefully planned words he had arranged to set before her. They had fled and left his soul bare before her gaze. He had nothing to tell but the story of himself.

"You think I have deceived you," he said, speaking rapidly because his heart was going in great, quick bounds; "and because I owe to you all the good that I have in life I have come to tell you the whole truth about myself. I thank you for having given me a few minutes to speak to you, and I will try not to weary you. I have been too much trouble to you already.

"I was a little lonely boy when my mother died—" Christie lowered his head as he talked now, and the firelight played fanciful lights and shades with the richness of his hair.

"Nobody loved me that I know of, unless it was my father. If he did, he never showed it. He was a silent man, and grieved about my mother's death. I was a homely little fellow, and they have always said I had the temper of my hair. My aunt used to say I was hard to manage. I think that was true. I must have had some love in my heart, but nothing but my mother ever called it forth. I went through school at war with all my teachers. I got through because I naturally liked books.

"Father wanted me to be a farmer, but I wanted to go to college; so he gave me a certain sum of money and sent me. I used the money as I pleased, sometimes wisely and sometimes unwisely. When I got out of money, I earned some more or went without it. Father was not the kind of man to be asked for more. I had a good time in college, though I can't say I ranked as well as I might have done. I studied what I pleased, and left other things alone. Father died before I graduated, and the aunt who kept house for him soon followed; and, when I was through college, I had no one to go to and no one to care where I went.

"Father had signed a note for a man a little before he died, with the usual result of such things, and there was very little remaining for him to leave to me. What there was I took and came to Florida, having a reckless longing to see a new part of the world, and make a spot for myself. I never had known what home was since I was a little fellow, and I believe I was homesick for a home and something to call my own. Land was cheap, and it was easy to work, I thought, and my head was filled with dreams of my future; but I soon saw that oranges did not grow in a day and produce fortunes.

"Life was an awfully empty thing. I used sometimes to lie awake at night and wonder what death would be, and if it wouldn't be as well to try it. But something in my mother's prayer for me when I was almost a baby always kept me from it. She used to pray, 'God make my little Chris a good man.'

"I began to get acquainted with a lot of other fellows in the same fix with myself after a while. They were all sick of life,—at least, the life down here, and hard work and interminable waiting. But they had found something pleasanter than death to make them forget.

"I went with them, and tried their way. They played cards. I played, too. I could play well. We would drink and drink, and play and drink again—"

A little moan escaped from the listener, and Christie looked up to find her eyes filled with tears and her fingers clutching the arms of the chair till the nails were pink against the finger-tips with the pressure.

"O, I am doing you more harm!" exclaimed Christie. "I will stop!"

"No, no," said Hazel. "Go on, please;" and she turned her face aside to brush away the tears that had gathered.

"I was always ashamed when it was over. It made me hate myself and life all the more. I often used to acknowledge to myself that I was doing about as much as I could to see that my mother's prayer didn't get answered. But still I went on just the same way every little while. There didn't seem to be anything else to do.

"Then the night before Christmas came. It wasn't anything to me more than any other day. It never had been since I was a mere baby. Mother used to fill my stocking with little things. I remember it just once.

"But this Christmas I felt particularly down. The orange-trees were not doing as well as I had hoped. I was depressed by the horror of the monotony of my life, behind and before. Then your things came, and a new world opened before me.

"I wasn't very glad of it at first. I am afraid I resented your kindness a little. Then I began to see the something homelike they had brought with them, and I could not help liking it. But your letter gave me a queer feeling. There seemed to be obligations I could not fulfil. I didn't like to keep the things, because you wanted a Sunday school. I was much more likely to conduct a saloon or a pool-room at that time than a Sunday school.

"Then I hung that picture up. You know what effect it had upon me. I have told you of my strange dream or vision or whatever it was. Yes, it was all true. I never deceived you about that or anything else except that I did not tell you I was not what you supposed. I thought it might embarrass you if I did so at first, and then it seemed but a joke to answer you as if I were a girl. I never dreamed it would go beyond that first letter when I wrote thanking you."

His honest eyes were on her face, and Hazel could not doubt him.

"And then, when the writing went on, and the time came when I ought to have told you, there was something else held me back. Forgive me for speaking of it, but I am trying to be perfectly true to-night. You remember in that second letter that you wrote me, where you told me that you were praying for me, and—you—" Christie caught his breath, and murmured the words low and reverently, "You said you loved me—"

"Oh!" gasped Hazel, clasping her white hands over her face, while the blood rushed up to her very high temples and surged around her little seashell ears.

Chapter 12

The Whim Completes Its Justification

"Forgive me!" he pleaded. "It need not hurt you. I knew that love was not really mine. It was given to the girl you thought I was. I knew without ever having seen you that you would sooner have cut out your tongue than write anything like that to a strange man. I ought to have seen at once that I was stealing something that did not belong to me in appropriating that love.

"Perhaps I would not have put it from me even if I had seen it. For that love was very dear to me. Remember I had never been loved in the whole of my life by any one but a mother who had been gone such years! Remember there was no one else to claim that love from you.

"And remember I thought that you would never need to know. I never dreamed that you would try to search me out. Your friendship was too dear to me for me to dare to try; and, too, I knew you would consider me far beneath you. I could never hope to have you for the most distant friend, even if you had known all about me from childhood.

"My hope for your help and comfort and friendship was in letting you suppose me a lonely old maid. Remember you said it yourself. I simply did not tell you what I was.

"But I do not take one bit of blame from myself. I see now that I ought to have been a good enough man to have told you at once. I should have missed a great deal, perhaps, as human vision sees it, have missed even heaven itself, unless the very giving up of heaven for right had gained heaven for me.

"I can see it was all wrong. The Father even then had spoken to my heart. He would have found me in some other way, perhaps; and it would have been your doing all the same, and I should have had the joy of thanking you even so for my salvation. But I did not, and now my punishment is that I have brought this suffering and disappointment and chagrin upon you. And if I could I would now be willing to wipe out of my life all the joy that has come to me through companionship with you by letters, if by so doing I might save you from this annoyance.

"For I have one more thing to tell you, and I will ask you to remember that I have never but once, in so many words, dared to tell you this in writing, and then only in a hidden way, because I thought if you knew all about me you would wish me not to say it. But now I must tell it. The punishment to me is very great, not only that you suffer, but that I have merited your scorn—for I love you! I love you with every bit of unused love from all my childhood days, in addition to all the love that a man's heart has to give. I have loved you ever since the night I read from your letter that you loved me—a poor, forlorn, homely girl as you thought—and that you thought I loved you too; and I knew at once that it was so.

"I want you to know that since that night I have had it ever before me to be a person worthy of loving you. I never dared put it 'worthy of your love,' because I knew that could never be for me. But I have tried to make myself a man such as you would not be ashamed to have love you, even though you could never think of loving in return. And I have fallen short in your eyes, I know. But in what you did not know of my life I have been true.

"Can you, knowing all this, forgive me? Then I shall go out and try to live my life as you and God would have me do, and remember the joy which was not mine. But you gave me one joy that you cannot take away. Jesus Christ is my Friend.

"Now I have said all there is to say, and I must go away and let you rest. Can you find it in your heart to say you forgive me?"

Christie rested his elbow on the arm of the chair, and dropped his head on his hand, while the firelight flickered and glowed among the waves of ruddy hair again. He had said all there was to say, and he felt he had no hope. Now he must go forth. The strength seemed suddenly to have left him.

It was very still in the room for a moment. They could hear each other breathe. At last Hazel's little white hand fluttered timidly out toward him, and rested like a rose-leaf among the dark curls.

It was his benediction, he thought, his dream come true. It was her forgiveness. He held his breath, and dared not stir.

And then, more timidly still, Hazel herself slipped softly from her chair to her knees before him. The other hand shyly stole to his shoulder, and she whispered: "Christie, forgive ME. I—love—*you.*"

Then Hazel's courage gave way, and she hid her blushing face against his sleeve.

Christie's heart leaped forth in all its manhood. He arose and drew her to her feet tenderly, and, folding his arms about her as one might infold an angel come for shelter, he bent his tall head over till his face touched her lily face, and he felt that all his desolation was healed.

There were steps along the hall that instant, lingering noisily about the door, and a hand rattling the door-knob, while Victoria's voice, unnecessarily loud from Ruth's point of view, called: "Is that you, Ruth? Are the others through dinner yet? Would you mind stepping back to the office and getting the evening paper for me? I want to look at something."

Then the door opened, and Victoria came smiling in. "Time's up," she said playfully. "The invalid must not talk another word to-night."

Indeed, Victoria was most relieved that the time was up, and she looked anxiously from Hazel to Christie to see whether she had done more harm that good; but Hazel leaned back smiling and flushed in her chair, and Christie, standing tall and grave with an uplifted look upon his face, reassured her.

She led him away by another hall than that the family would come up by, and was in so much hurry to get him away without being seen that she scarcely said a word to him. However, he did not know it.

"Well, is it all right?" she laughed nervously as they reached the side doorway.

"It is all right," he said with a joyous ring in his voice.

Through the hall, out the door, and down the steps went Christie Bailey, his hat in his hand, his face exalted, the moonlight "laying on his head a kingly crown." He felt that he had been crowned that night, crowned with a woman's love.

"He looks as if he had seen a vision," thought Victoria as she sped back to "view the ruins," as she expressed it to herself.

But Christie went on, his hat in his hand, down the long white road, looking up to the stars among the pines, wondering at the greatness of the world and the graciousness of God, on to his little cabin no longer filled with loneliness, and knelt before the pictured Christ and cried, "O my Father, I thank Thee."

Quite early in the morning Hazel requested a private interview with her father.

Now it was a well-acknowledged fact that Judge Winship was completely under his daughter's thumb; and, as the interview was a prolonged one, it was regarded as quite possible by the rest of the family party that there might be almost anything, from the endowment of a college settlement to a trip to Africa, in process of preparation; and all awaited the result with some restlessness.

But after dinner there were no developments. Hazel seemed bright and ready to sit on the piazza and be read to. Judge Winship took his umbrella and sauntered out for a walk, having declined the company of the various members of his family. Mother Winship calmed her anxieties, and concluded to take a nap.

Christie had gone about his morning tasks joyously. Now and again his heart questioned what he had to hope for in the future, poor as he was; but he put this resolutely down. He would rejoice in the knowledge of Hazel's forgiveness and her love, even though it never brought him anything else than that joy of knowledge.

In this frame of mind he looked forward exultantly to the Sunday-school hour. The young men when they came in wondered what had come over him, and the scholars greeted their superintendent with furtive nods and smiles.

During the opening of the Sunday school there came in an elderly gentleman of fine presence with iron-gray hair and keen blue eyes that looked piercingly out from under black brows. Christie had been praying when he came in. Christie's prayers were an index to his life. During the singing of the next hymn the superintendent came back to the door to give a book to the stranger, and, pausing in hesitation a moment, asked half shyly, "Will you say a few words to us, or pray?"

"Go on with your regular lesson, young man. I'm not prepared to speak. I'll pray at the close if you wish me to," said the stranger; and

Christie went back to his place, somewhat puzzled and embarrassed by the unexpected guest.

He lingered after all were gone, having asked that he might have a few words with Christie alone. Christie noticed that Mortimer had bowed to him in going out, and that he looked back curiously once or twice.

"My name is Winship," said the Judge brusquely. "I understand, young man, that you have told my daughter that you love her."

The color softly rose in Christie's temples till it flooded his whole face, but a light of love and of daring came into his eyes as he answered the unexpected challenge gravely, "I do, sir."

"Am I to understand, sir, by that, that you wish to marry her?"

Christie caught his breath. Hope and pain came quickly to defy one another. He stood still, not knowing what to say. He realized his helplessness, his unfitness for the love of Hazel Winship.

"Because," went on the relentless Judge, "in my day it was considered a very dishonorable thing to tell a young woman you loved her unless you wished to marry her; and, if you do not, I wish to know at once.

Christie was white now and humiliated.

"Sir," he said sternly, "I mean nothing dishonorable. I honor and reverence your daughter, yes, and love her, next to Jesus Christ," and involuntarily his eyes met those of the picture on the wall, "whom she has taught me to love. But, as your daughter has told you of my love, she must have also made you acquainted with the circumstances under which I told it to her. Had I not been trying to clear myself from a charge of deceit in her eyes, I should never have let her know the deep love I have for her; for I have nothing to offer her but my love. Judge Winship, is this the kind of home to offer to your daughter? It is all I have."

There was something pathetic, almost tragic, in the wave of Christie's hand as he looked around the cabin.

"Well, young man, it's a more comfortable place than my daughter's father was born in. There are worse homes than this. But perhaps you are not aware that my daughter will have enough of her own for two."

Christie threw his head back proudly, his eyes flashing bravely, though his voice was sad: "Sir, I will never be supported by my wife. If she comes to me, she comes to the home I can offer her; and it would have to be here, now, until I can do better."

"As you please, young man," answered the Judge shortly; but there was a grim smile upon his lips, and his eyes twinkled as if he were pleased. "I like your spirit. From all I hear of you you are quite worthy of her. She thinks so, anyway, which is more to the point. Have you enough to keep her from starving if she did come?"

"O, yes," Christie almost laughed in his eagerness. "Do you think—O, it *can*not be—that she would come?"

"She will have to settle that question," said her father, rising. "You have my permission to talk with her about it. As far as I can judge, she seems to have a fondness for logs with the bark on them. Good afternoon, Mr. Bailey. I am glad to have met you. You had a good Sunday school, and I respect you."

Christie gripped his hand until the old man almost cried out with the pain; but he bore it, grimly smiling, and went on his way.

And Christie, left alone in his little, glorified room, knelt once more, and called joyously: "My Father! My Father!"

* * *

"This is perfectly ridiculous," said Ruth Summers looking dismally out of the fast-flying car-window at the vanishing oaks and pines. "The wedding guests going off on the bridal tour, and the bride and bridegroom staying behind. I can't think whatever has possessed Hazel. Married in white cashmere under a tree, and not a single thing belonging to a wedding, not even a wedding breakfast—"

"You forget the wedding march," said Victoria, a vision of the organist's fine head coming to her, "and the strawberries for breakfast."

"A wedding march on that old organ," sneered Ruth, "with a row of black children for audience, and white sand for a background. Well, Hazel was original, to say the least. I hope she'll settle down now, and do as other people do."

"She won't," said Victoria positively. "She'll keep on having a perfectly lovely time all her life. Do you remember how she once said she was going to take Christie Bailey to Europe? Well, I reminded her of it this morning, and she laughed, and said she had not forgotten it; it was one thing she married him for, and he looked down at her wonderingly and asked what was that. How he does worship her!"

"Yes, and she's perfectly infatuated with him. I'm sure one would have to be, to live in a shanty. I don't believe I could love any man enough for that," she said reflectively, studying the back of Tom Winship's well-trimmed head in the next seat.

"Then you'd better not get married," said Victoria. She looked dreamily out of the window at the hurrying palmettos and added: "One might—if one loved enough;" and then she was silent, thinking of a promise that had been made her, a promise of better things, signed by a true look from a pair of handsome, courageous eyes.

Christie and Hazel watched the fast-flying train as it vanished from their sight, and then turned slowly toward their home.

"It is a palace to me now that you are in it, my wife!" Christie pronounced the words with wonder and awe.

"You dear old organ, it was you that did it all," said Hazel, touching the keys tenderly, and turning to Christie with tears of joy standing in her eyes she put her hands in his and said, "My husband."

Then as if by common consent they knelt together, hand in hand, beneath the picture of the Christ, and Christie prayed; and now his prayer began, "Our Father."